UNEASY ALLIANCE

Joanne is intelligent, capable — and beautiful. Her female colleagues always assume this plays a major part in her rapid promotions, no matter where she works, and now all she has to show for her efforts is her current state of unemployment and a string of short-lived jobs on her CV. Signing up with an exclusive dating agency, she meets tycoon Benedict North — an exceptional, charismatic man. But when she finally lands a job, Joanne is unsure of whether there is room in her life for him — despite her growing feelings . . .

WENDY KREMER

UNEASY ALLIANCE

Complete and Unabridged

LINFORD
Leicester

First published in Great Britain in 2015

First Linford Edition
published 2016

A catalogue record for this book is available
from the British Library.

ISBN 978–1–4448–3056–9

Published by
F. A. Thorpe (Publishing)
Anstey, Leicestershire

Set by Words & Graphics Ltd.
Anstey, Leicestershire
Printed and bound in Great Britain by
T. J. International Ltd., Padstow, Cornwall

This book is printed on acid-free paper

1

Joanne looked out of the window into the darkness, and at the walls of the underground whizzing past. She mused that her life and its objectives seemed to be passing by just as fast. She'd always believed that after she left university with a first-class degree, she'd automatically find herself a good job, and then other things — like meeting someone special, owning her own flat, a car — would all fall magically into place. It hadn't happened like that at all.

She'd worked for several companies since leaving university. She hadn't yet found the right job because, up until now, other women disliked the amount of attention men gave her, and men didn't like discovering that she was a competitor for any promotion chances. After a couple of weeks, she was usually running circles around her co-workers.

She didn't set out to challenge anyone's position; she was just good at her job, and her superiors noticed it. People who'd been there longer clearly resented it, and begrudged her swift advancement. The atmosphere usually worsened, and she was too sensitive to tolerate the initial stages of mobbing, so she quit. She always seemed to be the first to lose her job when there were dismissals, although in fairness, the most recent job-loss had been a genuine case of 'last in, first out'.

After too many new starts, she was beginning to doubt her own abilities. At interviews for any new job, prospective employers wrinkled their brows and gave her questioning looks as they surveyed the long list of previous employment on her CV. Colleen, her oldest and best friend, had advised her to leave some of them off, but Joanne reasoned that if anyone did check carefully, they'd stumble across the truth, and that would look even worse. Feeling miserable and dejected, she mused that it seemed to be impossible to find a permanent job where she could use her skills without having to face stumbling blocks all the time.

Offering her a bag of sweets on their ride home, Colleen said, 'Your trouble is your looks. Blokes fancy you until the moment they realize you're just as clever as them — more so, usually. And you won't pretend to be dumb.'

Joanne tossed her head. 'I can't pretend that I'm not as clued-up as they are. Why should I? It goes against the grain to do that. I don't think I could sit in the corner and twiddle my thumbs, or shove papers around my desk all day without getting anywhere.'

Colleen laughed. 'You're too honest. You should be like me, and just lull your colleagues into a false sense of security! They think I'm content to remain in my little corner and cope with whatever they throw at me. They think I'm harmless, so they never make any attempt to hoist me out. In time, my bosses notice I do my work well and unobtrusively, and come to the conclusion that I deserve to move up the ladder and be promoted. *Et voila!*'

Joanne smiled. 'Devious! I wish I could bite my tongue or feign silliness, but I can't. Remember what it was like in school? Everyone so resentful, just because I got good exam results. They nicknamed me 'swotty', or worse!'

'You assumed everyone was resentful, but the truth is, the majority did like you; and the boys fancied you, even in those days. The unintelligent ones were the lot who called you names. It was a well-known fact that you would willingly help anyone who asked. Gaynor Smith only got through her maths exam because you coached her for weeks beforehand. You let us all copy your homework if we hadn't done it — even if you got into trouble for it — and you never boasted. Look at us two! We've always got on like a house on fire, despite the fact that I only have a run-of-the-mill degree and less than half your ambition. You've got everything going for you: looks and brains! Why don't you just steamroller people?

Walk over a few dead bodies to get to your goal, if that's what you need to do. Wear blinkers, and ignore people who annoy you on the way.'

Joanne laughed. 'I've tried to ignore people, but it doesn't work. It just makes me unhappy to know I'm disliked. I wish I were like you. You're so contented and happy-go-lucky. No one would ever peg you as work-orientated.'

'Ah! But I am — in a less obvious way, darling. My colleagues are unaware that they are being manipulated. I may not have such a super brain or be as good-looking as you, but we all have to make the best of what we've got. It would make a world of difference if you just relaxed and didn't analyse every move before you made it. I think you expect the worst to happen each time you start a new job — and then, of course, it does.'

Joanne's brows lifted and she eyed her friend with an anxious expression. 'Please don't tell me you're fed up with all my moaning and are going to dump me too?'

Colleen chuckled and her dark eyes twinkled. 'I'll never dump you. Remember how we became blood sisters all those years ago?'

Joanne winced. 'I remember we used a rusty penknife; I still think it was a miracle that neither of us got blood poisoning!'

Colleen put her arm round her friend's shoulder. 'See what I mean? I just remember that it made us sisters for life! Something good will turn up for you soon, I'm sure it will.'

'I wish I was as optimistic. There's no job on the horizon, and my savings are perilously low. I won't be able to keep up the rent on my flat indefinitely. I don't intend to burden Mum and Dad either, now that they're retired. They deserve to enjoy life at last. They shouldn't have to worry about supporting their grown-up daughter. I haven't yet told them that I'm out of a job again.'

The sweet bag rustled as Colleen pushed it haphazardly back into her bag. 'You know, if the worst comes to the worst, you can always move in with me.'

'That's lovely of you, thank you, but I have to stand on my own feet. I'm praying I'll find a regular job soon. I'm prepared to fill shelves, or stand behind a stall in a market selling parsnips and potatoes, or deliver the morning paper. I'll do anything that brings in some regular money.'

'Those kinds of jobs don't pay much. You'd have to take on two or three of them just to make ends meet. Are you quite sure you don't want me to ask my boss if there's an opening with us?'

Joanne shook her head and her copper hair swung in heavy waves around her face. 'No way! If I caused disruption in your office, it might boomerang and get you into trouble for recommending me. I have to find something on my own.'

Colleen looked up. 'My stop coming up. Want to come to an exhibition of Georgian furniture at the Sutton Gallery tomorrow evening? It might take your mind off your troubles.'

Joanne sighed and shook her head. 'I can't afford to go to any exhibitions, and I'm not as wild about antique furniture, as you are. You know that very well.'

'But you humour me constantly by coming along when I ask. I'll treat you.'

Sounding quite determined, Joanne replied, 'If I can't pay my own way, I won't come. Although, thank you for asking me. When I have a steady income, I'll come with you to as many exhibitions, displays and expositions as you like. Promise!'

'Well, why don't you at least come home with me now? We can have something to eat and a night in with the telly.'

Joanne shook her head. 'Thanks, but you know I hate travelling on the underground late at night.'

Colleen grabbed her bag and stood up as the train approached her destination. She looked down at her friend and smiled. Joanne certainly did stand out in a crowd with that hair, and those beautiful green eyes. She'd been blessed by the gods, or cursed, whichever way you looked at it. 'We'll get together on Saturday, as usual?'

Joanne nodded. 'Of course.'

The doors slid open and Colleen skipped out onto the platform. With another quick glance in Joanne's direction, she joined the stream of people heading for the exit. The doors closed and the train set off for the next stop.

Joanne leaned back and wished there really was something promising to look forward to on the horizon. She couldn't think of anything. Instead, she tried to focus on the good things in her life — her friendship with Colleen, her family. And there was their wider circle of friends too, of course — the people she and Colleen had known for years and sometimes met on the weekend. Although she couldn't afford to see them too often these days.

The train was slowing down again, and she got up. Not so many people got out here. She hoisted her bag and stepped outside. She wasn't in as much of a hurry as the others leaving the train, and she looked around casually before she walked towards the exit. An advertisement on the wall caught her attention. It was promoting the services of an exclusive dating agency. She stopped in her tracks, and a man in city garb almost ran into her.

'Sorry!' she muttered, and stepped aside. The train left and the platform was soon empty, apart from her, staring at the advertisement stuck on the wall. Could this be a temporary solution to her present dilemma? They probably paid well, and from the style and the wording, it did look to be quite exclusive. It might be some kind of dubious call-girl business, but if it were a genuine, exclusive agency, and she could get onto their lists, it would help to pay her rent until she had a proper job. Everyone always said she had above-average looks, and she had a university degree. They were both things that might impress a well-to-do client. She'd phone to find out more; that wouldn't commit her in any way. She took a note of the contact details and went on. She'd tell Colleen about it, after she knew what kind of agency it was. Colleen was right! She should be a bit more venturesome.

Two days later, she was sitting opposite a smart, middle-aged woman named Mrs Partridge. She wore a chic, black sheath dress with three-quarter length sleeves. There was a string of pearls round her neck. Mrs Partridge shuffled the papers on the desktop and, after she viewed the top sheet briefly again, she said, 'I hope you realize that the Partridge Agency is a very exclusive firm, Miss Courtland? This is not a sleazy, back street concern. We are a serious enterprise, offering temporary companions specifically for social events, and our clients are top society.'

Joanne cleared her throat. 'Yes, I understand that. From what you told me on the telephone, it entails partnering your client for a single evening and no further contact after that?'

The older woman patted her grey hair on the side and looked over the top of her half-glasses.

'That's exactly right. We don't encourage repeat contact. We provide a partner for a one-off occasion. Usually, it's because the client needs a plus-one for some kind of event, but doesn't want the hassle of finding someone suitable. We are definitely not an agency for people who think they can use us as a way of finding themselves a rich, prominent spouse. It goes without saying that we expect extreme discretion on both sides.'

Joanne nodded.

Mrs Partridge looked at the papers again, then removed her spectacles and studied Joanne for a moment.

'And why have you suddenly decided to come to us, Miss Courtland? I see that you are highly qualified. Why are you not using your qualifications to find yourself a job suited to your education and skills?'

There was no reason Joanne couldn't be direct.

'My appearance seems to have had a negative effect on my employment prospects so far. I'm not sure if I've imagined it, but I think it's often been the case.' She shrugged her shoulders. 'The men are okay, as long as they think my looks are my only real qualification. The women are friendly, as long as they don't feel I'm getting too much attention. When co-workers find out I'm good at my job, they often start being bitchy or hostile. My savings are dwindling fast, and I need to earn money soon, otherwise I'm in danger of losing my flat. I've been trying to find a new job for a couple of weeks now — and I intend to go on trying — but when I spotted your advertisement, it sounded like it could be a temporary solution for me.' She met the other woman's glance. 'I wouldn't agree to be a bed-partner, so if that is part of the agreement, we needn't waste each other's time.'

Mrs Partridge stiffened visibly. 'I can assure you, we are not that kind of an agency. Our companions are handpicked for their diplomacy and tact, and our clients are top notch. The contract most definitely does not include a romp between the sheets.'

Joanne hastened to explain. 'I wasn't trying to be offensive, I just wanted to be clear.'

Mrs Partridge nodded. 'Well, you have the necessary intelligence and looks. Did you bring a photo?'

Joanne took an envelope out of her bag. 'This studio portrait was taken last Christmas. I had it done as a present for my parents.' She handed it across the desk and Mrs Partridge adjusted her glasses again.

'Hmm! It doesn't do you justice, but it gives the client a good idea. I won't add you to our comprehensive list; that can entail accompanying clients abroad sometimes, and from what you've said, you might not be available. As you are looking for temporary work until you find permanent employment, I will put you down as only being prepared to attend events in London. I can't promise that

14

we'll have an assignment come up for you before you find new employment. It depends very much on a client's personal taste.'

'Yes, that's alright. I understand completely.'

'You'll need attractive evening attire and accessories if someone asks for you.'

'That's no problem.' Joanne crossed her fingers. She didn't have anything that was suitable for an exclusive do, but she'd cross that bridge when she came to it. She cleared the frog in her throat. 'And the payment?'

Mrs Partridge mentioned an amount for a single assignment.

Joanne's eyes widened. 'Just for one evening?'

Mrs Partridge nodded. 'As I explained, our clients are exclusive, and they pay for absolute discretion and tact. Our contract contains a clause threatening legal and financial reprisals if the press or any other source is informed about the real state of affairs. I have to trust my employees, down to the last comma. If they don't stick to the rules, it'd be financial ruin, for them and me. I'm sure that a lot of our clients have enough power to make anyone's life extremely uncomfortable at the time and thereafter, if they choose to do so.'

'I know it doesn't really make any difference,' said Joanne, 'but I wonder why they need to pay someone for company in the first place. If they come from affluent, influential circles, surely there's never any lack of hangers-on who'd be happy to accommodate.'

Mrs Partridge smiled softly for the first time, and shrugged. 'I expect that's precisely the point. It's easier for our clients to pay for an intelligent companion for an event, and have it remain a limited, contractually-bound agreement. An individual from their own social circle may well hope it's the start of a lasting relationship. If that doesn't happen, disappointment can turn to bitterness. I make it a rule never to ask why clients wish to employ a companion. I just know

16

they don't want to go somewhere solo, and are avoiding socialites and social climbers.'

'It's still strange though, isn't it? When normal people, like me, haven't got a boyfriend or a girlfriend to go to an event with, all one needs is a good friend who'll fill the gap in an emergency. Why is it so different for your clients?'

Mrs Partridge's eyes twinkled. 'I think their actions are usually governed by rational reasoning. A 'good friend', as you put it, might be inclined to get the wrong idea after a while, and then it is back to square one again. We are anonymous. Perhaps a client just thinks sensibly about trying to keep his or her private life just that — private. Perhaps it's less complicated to pay for discreet company now and then, than to endanger a genuine relationship by putting a partner into the limelight too soon. It can also serve the purpose of putting the media off the scent.'

'If I was someone's girlfriend, I don't think I'd put up with him flaunting another woman in the limelight while I was hidden in the wings. I hope the press won't plaster my name across the headlines if I do get an assignment?'

Mrs Partridge laughed softly, got up, and held out her hand. 'I promise you, it's not very likely that you'll get into the newspapers. In fact, I can't remember it ever occurring. Even if the press gets wind of a new 'romance', a good PR department denies the individual was anyone special, and they can't be bothered. They need gossip. It is much more rewarding to print about a celebrity who was found drunk and half-unconscious on the toilet floor of a West End club than research an unknown face and an unknown name. I'll put you on our lists, and if someone picks you out, I'll be in touch. I have your contact details?'

'Yes, all there, on the back of the photo.' Joanne shook her hand.

After a second, the older woman considered her closely, and said, 'It's just a thought, but why don't you look

18

for a job with a small company? Somewhere you'd be in charge of the office. It would mean more involvement and effort on your part, but somehow, I don't think you'd mind any extra work.'

Joanne looked at her. 'Do you know, I've never thought of that? It's a very good idea. I've always focussed on big companies. After leaving university, you automatically think that's the only way to go. A small company wouldn't pay as much, but I'm looking for permanent work and a steady income at the moment. As long as I earn enough to cover my basic needs, I'd be happy, even if the company isn't a global player. I don't need a fantastic salary, just a reasonable one. Thanks for the suggestion!'

'You're welcome, and I wish you luck. If you do find something, you will get in touch so that I can take you off our books again?'

'Yes, promise! Thank you for the interview.'

Joanne left the office and Mrs Partridge smiled after her. She liked her, and almost hoped that the girl would find herself a permanent job, even though she was an excellent addition to her lists, and had a very good chance of being chosen.

2

Following Mrs Partridge's suggestion, Joanne had spent her time applying for jobs with smaller firms, and there had been pleasing results. She was hoping to hear back from a small building company and had just spotted a vacancy for a job within walking distance of her flat. Both positions needed someone to run an office single-handed. That sounded promising. She didn't know yet what was involved, and hoped, if it got that far, the interviewers wouldn't take one look at her, think she was empty-headed and dismiss her without giving her a chance. Joanne kept her fingers crossed.

She was on her way to post some letters when Mrs Partridge phoned. When they finished their conversation, Joanne felt slightly dazed. Mrs Partridge had just told her she'd been engaged for Friday evening — in three days' time.

The man was called Benedict North. It was scarcely a week since she'd been for the interview at the agency.

She rang Colleen. After explaining briefly, Joanne said, 'So, where can I get an expensive-looking evening dress, for a reasonable price? Any idea?'

Colleen squealed. 'Good heavens! You've been picked already? Do you know anything about the man?'

'Just his name. Mrs Partridge says she'll send me an email with more details. What about a dress, any ideas?'

There was a moment's silence. 'Hmm! Obviously you can't afford to buy a new one, and I've nothing suitable that would fit you. I'll go and ask Gloria in Accounts. She's a party queen and I expect she'll know. I'll call you back in a couple of minutes. Where are you?'

'I'm on my way back from posting off another lot of applications.'

'Right! Keep your phone turned on.'

Joanne walked on. It was a bright, cheerful day. The trees were beginning to lose their leaves and the pavement bordering the local playing field was already carpeted with them. Their glorious reds and golds were something from a picture postcard. For the first time in weeks, she felt optimistic and cheerful. Joanne kicked up the leaves as she went along, and she smiled to herself. She stopped for a moment to watch a group of schoolchildren playing hockey. They were having a great time. Their voices, and that of their teacher, drifted across the playing field towards her.

Her phone rang again. 'Joanne? I've just spoken to Gloria, and she suggested you either go to a shop that sells second-hand designer clothes — she gave me the address of the one she uses — or go to a dress-hire company. She gave me the address of one of those too.'

'That sounds good. I'm almost home. Can you email me the addresses? I could check them out this afternoon. I haven't got anything better to do anyway. Can you pass on my thanks to Gloria, and thank you too. You're a saviour!'

'This is so exciting! It should be fun.'

'I wouldn't call it fun, exactly. I don't know the man, or what he does; I don't know what kind of event it is, or why he needs to pay a complete stranger to be his partner.'

'It's probably like that woman explained. He doesn't want commitment or complications. Check him out on the Internet before you go. You might even find out what event he's due to attend, if you're lucky. Some company websites give details about forthcoming social events. And remember, on the actual date, you can always scarper if you think things are going off-rail.'

Joanne laughed. 'You're right, but it's me and not you, who has to face Mr Anonymous.'

'Call me later to tell me what you find out about him — and how you got on with finding a dress.'

Back at the flat, Joanne checked her computer. As promised, there was an email from the Partridge Agency, and another from Colleen with the addresses. She was too curious not to open the agency one straight away. She was to meet Benedict North in the foyer of a hotel in the West End, where the event was taking place. She read through the details, and then opened an attachment giving her more information about the man himself. It was an impressive summary of achievements. She suddenly realized she already knew the name from the financial sections of the newspapers. He was well known in business circles, and the company headquarters was in the city. It had numerous national and international subordinate companies too. From the details in Mrs Partridge's info, he'd built it up from scratch. Benedict North was single, thirty-six, lived in London, but was constantly on the move, juggling the management of the various companies. There wasn't much personal information about him, and there was no photo either. Joanne wanted to recognize him straight away and understand enough about his company structures to sound knowledgeable.

She entered his name into her search

engine, and was rewarded with several pages covering his various companies. After skimming through some of them, she found a photo of him and leaned back in her chair to consider it.

Benedict North was posed against the background of one of his company buildings in the city. It was a very good photo. He stood with shoulders back, in a formal business suit, and gazed, unperturbed, at the camera. He was tall and well proportioned. His facial features were strong. His mouth was unsmiling and wide, and there was a cleft in his chin. His nose was long and narrow, and his shadowed eyes seemed heavy-lidded. Joanne tried to assess the man's personality as she regarded the photo. It was an interesting face — not outstandingly handsome, but thought provoking There was something about his direct gaze that caught her attention. His eyes dominated his expression, and the set of his shoulders indicated he was probably a bit stiff-necked and proud; but something about his mouth told her he also possessed humour, possibly of a mocking sort. Undoubtedly, he didn't suffer fools gladly — no one in his position got there by being easy-going and undemanding, and if he set himself high standards, he most likely expected the same thing from friends and employees alike.

Joanne viewed him with a lively interest, and her curiosity was wakened. She guessed that his success was based on a determined, resolute character. His past and present achievements were probably the result of his single-minded willpower. At least he wasn't over fifty, with a potbelly. In fact, he was a lot more attractive than she expected. It could be an old photo, of course, but she guessed he had a public relations department somewhere that kept his personal website information up-to-date.

She glanced at her watch. She'd check through the rest of the information this evening. She had to concentrate on finding something appropriate to wear, and get it settled this afternoon if possible. She'd have to get a hair appointment before Friday too. She made herself a sandwich and, after donning her newest coat and shoes, she set off to check the first address on Colleen's list. It was in Chelsea.

* * *

When she reached the boutique, the shop was, outwardly, a small one. All the shops she had passed on the way down the street were similar, and she noted that they only displayed one or two items in the window, with no price tickets. She wondered how a second-hand shop could exist among others that offered exclusive fashion, but perhaps there was a kind of symbiosis. The second-hand shop provided a journey's end for wealthy customers to dispose of items they no longer wanted, without too much inconvenience, before they turned their attention to buying something new. A loud buzzer signalled somewhere in the back of the shop when she entered the thickly carpeted front section. A stiff-looking saleswoman with perfectly styled hair and a figure like a pencil came towards her.

'Can I help you?'

Joanne noticed how the woman's eyes were evaluating her clothes and general appearance. Joanne already felt uncomfortable, and she'd only just arrived. She cleared her throat.

'Someone recommended this shop to me. I'm looking for an evening dress for a special event this Friday.'

'I see. Do you need a cocktail dress, a short-length model or a floor-length one?'

'Being perfectly honest, I don't know.'

With a growing trace of vexation in her voice, she asked. 'Do you know where the event is being held?'

Joanne told her.

'Long. You definitely need long!' The woman turned away and, without further comment, moved towards racks lining the pale walls, displaying various types of dresses. It was clear she expected Joanne to follow.

'Any suitable dresses we have for an

event at that hotel will be among these.' She ran her hands along a rail holding numerous evening dresses, and then started to ruffle through the rack more carefully. 'Size?'

'Depending on the cut, ten or twelve.'

The saleswoman freed a shimmering gold sheath dress. 'This would suit you very well.' She threw another deceptively simple one in black, and another in coral with a halter neckline, over her arm. With a small smile, she offered the comment, 'Black will never be out of date for special occasions. The lady who put this one up for sale only did so because she now has too many blacks in her wardrobe. Plus, in certain circles, if you've worn something a couple of times, people notice, and you are forced to have to find replacements.' She laughed. 'Not that that's a punishment, for someone who has time on her hands and plenty of money, of course.'

Joanne's mouth felt dry. She wasn't in the right place. There was something too snobbish about the saleswoman's manner and artificial chatter.

The woman walked towards the back of the shop. Over her shoulder, she said. 'Why don't you try these on for starters? The length should be okay. You are about average height, and so were their previous owners. This way!'

The changing cubicle in the back of the shop was constricting. Joanne couldn't even turn round properly, and she was conscious that the saleswoman was waiting just outside the dividing curtain. Joanne hurried to divest herself of her clothes, then squeezed into the sequinned dress. It felt far too tight. She threw open the curtain to look at herself in the full-length mirror opposite. She looked like an overstuffed sausage. Joanne shook her head.

'Why not? It looks really good on you. The colour is just right.'

Without commenting, Joanne returned to the cubicle, changed quickly into the black, which fitted better but had a revealing neckline, and a hemline that dragged across the carpet.

The woman rested her chin in her hand and considered her. 'Perfect. You can't go wrong with that one.'

Tugging the neckline, Joanne felt her hostility mounting. 'Apart from anything else, it needs shortening, and the neckline is much too revealing. I don't like it at all.' Ignoring the saleswoman's sour expression, Joanne glanced at the coral dress, but made no move to try it on. Instead, she asked, 'How much do the dresses cost?'

'You don't want to try this one?' She held out the coral one still hanging over her arm.

Joanne shook her head, feeling more confident. 'That colour wouldn't suit me at all, I know that without even trying it on.' The woman was getting impatient, and Joanne already wanted to leave, although she'd only been in the shop for a short time. The saleswoman was clearly only interested in persuading her to buy something unsuitable. Probably she wanted to get rid of these particular dresses because they'd been around too long.

Adjusting the sequined version over her arm, the saleswoman mentioned prices that left Joanne breathless. She shook her head.

'Perhaps they look good on someone else, but they're not what I'm looking for. I couldn't afford them, even if I did like them! You have nothing else? Perhaps something that's not so expensive, in green or bronze?'

With a haughty expression, she shook her head. 'Not at the moment, I'm afraid.'

Joanne shrugged and returned to the cubicle. She changed quickly and wondered what the saleswoman would think about her Marks and Spencer underwear. She was still waiting when Joanne came out. Handing her the black dress, Joanne finished buttoning her coat and walked back to the sales area. Being as polite as she could, she murmured, 'Thank you anyway,' before she headed for the door. The saleswoman merely stared after her and pursed her lips even tighter.

Glad to be outside in the fresh air, Joanne wondered how Colleen's workmate could afford such prices. Perhaps if she was a regular customer, she got the pick of the less expensive items as soon as they arrived. Joanne straightened her shoulders and looked at the next address. If she didn't have more luck there, she'd have to think of another solution. Her bank account wouldn't permit her to make useless purchases and, at the moment, an evening dress was a useless purchase. Time was running out. She searched the crevices of her brain for someone who was roughly the same size, and possessed a great evening dress. No one sprang to mind.

★   ★   ★

Joanne found the dress-hire company easily. It was in a less exclusive area of the West End and down a side street. A bell tinkled as she pushed the door open. She was relieved to see the surroundings were smart, but also comfortable.

The reception area was stylish, with snug armchairs and a small counter tucked away in one of the corners. A young man appeared from somewhere out the back. He was dressed in a smart suit and white shirt. His appearance was just a touch too fussy to be defined as classical, and not fussy enough to be described as odd.

He looked at Joanne and asked politely, 'Can I help you?'

She explained. His expression brightened.

'Thank heavens! You're exactly what I need to cheer me up. I've just got rid of a family who wanted to hire stuff for a wedding. It was hell! The men didn't know what they wanted, and their wives were looking at things that were totally unsuitable. Instead of sticking to simple lines and colours, it turned into a real battle between the two sisters about whether to choose pink or lilac.' Clearly on a roll, he went on, 'When I asked about what the bridesmaids were wearing, I nearly fell off my perch when they said 'orange'! It took all of my tact and persuasion to make them realize yellow or a very elegant silver grey would be better.' He smiled at her. 'I'm lucky I haven't got a raging headache after three hours of that lot. But now you're here, I'm all set to enjoy searching through our racks to find you just what you want.'

Joanne laughed softly. This place was definitely much better. She relaxed noticeably.

He eyed her carefully, his hand cradling his chin. 'Long or short?'

'Long.'

'Elegant, showy, gaudy, or dazzling?'

'Elegant.'

'Figure-hugging or flowing?'

'Flowing, but shaped.'

He nodded. 'Preferred colours?'

'Green, black, or bronze. Or yellow, as long as it's not too bright.'

'You'd look good in dove, pale grey, or muted beige tones too, but for evening wear you need to be more dramatic. I think we have a couple of possibilities. Size ten?'

'Generally, but sometimes a twelve looks better.'

Nodding approvingly, he said, 'I love customers who are honest about their size. Follow me!'

He turned on his heel and she went after him into the rear of the shop. A glance around the room showed her they were in the section containing the male attire. Suits, coats, jackets, trousers, and various male accessories, populated long rows of racks and shelves right into the shadows at the far end. He was already climbing a spiral staircase on the side. The upper level was a place of delight for any female. Joanne immediately spotted wedding dresses, all kinds of formal and party dresses, suits, and other kinds of outdoor wear hanging in long rows in every colour of the rainbow. There were long tables holding handbags and matching shoes, scarves and costume jewellery, and a sprinkling of floor-length mirrors.

He made a sweeping gesture. 'As you can see, most of our clothes are formal dresses. Not many women these days would consider hiring a jacket or a two-piece business costume, although it does happen now and then. People want clothes from us they wouldn't normally buy because they know it's just for one special occasion; a wedding, a formal dance, that sort of thing. I'll pick out a couple of dresses I think would suit you, but you're welcome to wander around and see if you can find something that catches your eye.'

He left her and Joanne wandered among the rows, looking here and there whenever a colour caught her eye. The dresses and costumes were in protective coverings. Some had see-through coverings from the shoulder to the waist, and others, like the wedding dresses, had full-length protection. There was a wonderful choice, and she soon discovered she didn't know where to start. She was glad when he returned with a couple of dresses over his arm.

'Found anything you fancy?'

She smiled at him. 'There's too much. I'd need a lot more time to sort out something from this lot.'

He nodded understandingly. 'That's why I'm here. I love making suggestions. Sometimes it works, and sometimes not. Don't worry if you don't like the dresses I'm suggesting — no matter how many you reject, it all helps me to pinpoint your taste and narrow things down to the final choice. The changing rooms are over here.'

He led the way.

The next hour was one of the nicest she'd spent for a long time. They were soon on first-name terms with each other. Granville was very critical, and very helpful. Every telling, unsightly crease or clash of colour was commented on and pointed out. Joanne was sure he was being completely honest, and he was genuinely involved in finding her just what she wanted. She'd tried several possibilities, including a dark green silk sheath dress that suited her colouring to perfection, and she had almost settled on it when Granville turned up with another one in black that had a layer of diaphanous covering. He urged her to try it and she did.

It fitted like a glove and there was absolutely no need to hold her stomach in either. It flattered her figure and made her skin look like fine porcelain. It was high-necked, with long-length sheer sleeves that had been embroidered in the same motif as the rest of the gauzy surface. It dipped in the back, but not too far and Joanne felt comfortable yet glamorous in it. The skirt moved in flattering rhythm with her long strides, yet didn't drag.

He clapped his hands. 'That's it! The green one is fine, but that one looks absolutely great. If you wear a bit more make-up, and your hair down around your shoulders like now, it will look sensational. You need a clutch bag and comfortably high heels. Darling! Take a tip from Granville: never buy shoes that are not comfortable. Buy comfortable high-heels that are fun to wear; the good ones are expensive, but worth every penny, because you'll wear them all the time.'

'I have a glitzy black evening clutch bag and a pair of matching shoes in black. I also have a pashmina scarf that's extra long and wide. My mother brought it back from Singapore for me from their last holiday. I think it could serve as a wrap.'

He looked expectantly, but with a more critical expression. 'Colour?'

'Greys and silver. Swirls and leaves.'

'Sounds perfect.'

'Granville, I like it. I love it! But can I afford it?'

'I'll have to check, but I'm sure you can. If you return it within three days, it's cheaper than for five days or longer.' He looked around, although there was no one else in the building. 'I'll date it from tomorrow afternoon, so if you manage to bring it in on Saturday, you'll get the best deal. We always have the clothes dry-cleaned when they come back, it adds to the costs but it's the only way. Have another look at yourself in the mirror and when you're sure, change and come back downstairs. I'll find out just how much the whole caboodle costs in the meantime.'

Joanne found that it was still more expensive than expected, but she could afford it, especially when she thought about how much she would be earning. It was a beautiful dress, and it made her feel good. She handed Granville her credit card with a clear conscience.

With the dress packed between layers of tissue paper in a box, she looked back at him when she reached the door.

He grinned. 'Ciao Joanne! Have a great time. I'm look forward to hearing about how you wowed them all when you bring it back.'

3

Colleen had asked her latest boyfriend to give Joanne a lift, so she got to the hotel in plenty of time. She had two reasons to be grateful for the lift. Firstly, two taxi trips across half of London and back would take a huge chunk out of her fee, and secondly, the alternative would be to get there via the underground, and the prospect of doing so in an evening dress and a flimsy wrap wasn't tempting. She thanked Paul and got out. She'd met him several times, and even though she thought he wasn't right for Colleen, he seemed a nice enough chap, and she always tried to be friendly. He nodded, gave her a hasty smile, and drove off quickly, leaving her to join the stream of well-dressed people going into the hotel.

Joanne was nervous, but she hoped that she looked the part of a glamorous girlfriend. Her hair gleamed and rested in subtle waves around her shoulders. It swung gently with every movement of her head. Her make-up was more defined than usual, but wasn't over-done. She fingered her clutch bag uneasily and adjusted her wrap as she waited at the agreed meeting point, in the vicinity of the reception desk inside the hotel. He would know what she looked like from the agency photo, and she knew him from his photo on the Internet. The room was elegant, with long windows and high ceilings. The furniture was ultra modern, clearly expensive and comfortable, but no one was interested in sitting down at the moment.

He came towards her with determined strides and as he drew closer, she noticed a fleeting expression that made her wonder if he was now sorry that he'd made the arrangement with the agency. His face looked more mature than in the photo. Close up, she could see details, like the small lines at the corner of his grey eyes, that his face seemed thinner because his cheekbones and nose seemed more prominent than in the photo, and his expertly-cut hair was shorter. He was tall, and slightly built, and gave her the impression that he was someone who was disciplined and dynamic. There was something about his presence that made her understand why people in the business world warned competitors not to underestimate him.

He stopped in front of her, and looked down.

'Miss Courtland?'

'Mr North?'

He took her elbow. 'Let's move to the edge of this crush, so that I can tell you what I expect.'

Joanne blinked, but followed his lead. It wasn't surprising he wanted to clarify what he expected of her, and how she should act, but she had also hoped for a smile or two before they actually got down to brass tacks.

He found a quiet spot on the periphery and viewed her carefully.

'Steer clear of any personal remarks

about how we met, or where we stand. Don't comment on anything you know nothing about, and if you can't think of a suitable general comment about something, just nod and listen. That always works. People love to think you're agreeing with them, and they are usually satisfied if you nod your head, or just smile.'

She pulled herself together. 'What if people start talking about something to do with your personal life and they expect me to know all about it?'

The corner of his lips lifted a little, as if he was amused by the question.

'I would be very surprised if anyone mentions my personal life. Hardly anyone knows much about me, thank God. The only person present this evening that might do is Charles. We've known each other for years. He runs an extremely successful art gallery in Mayfair, and was responsible for the artwork in the new building. That's why he's here tonight. He's the only one who is likely to be curious enough to ask you personal questions — like where you come from, or what you do. He'll presume you know a lot more about me than you do, so play along with it. If he talks about something you're not sure about, try distracting him.' His gaze moved and lazily appraised her, from top to toe. 'I'm sure you know how to do that.'

Feeling like a prize cow in a market, her colour heightened. She swallowed hard and said, 'I don't particularly like that remark, or what it insinuates, Mr North.'

He glanced at her, a softer expression on his face, and surprised her with a sudden smile.

'Sorry. I didn't intend to be rude. I wasn't suggesting that you should distract him physically. I meant if nothing else worked, you'd need to distract him with a new topic of conversation. I'm not implying you're some kind of temptress. I know that the Partridge Agency is entirely above-board and legitimate. Someone recommended it, and I also checked it out personally beforehand.'

She grew hot and then cold and her

stomach tightened. She managed to control her annoyance, and her heightened colour receded a little. Even though her green eyes still sparkled dangerously, she tried to bring the conversation back to a normal level again.

'Then we both know what's expected. I gather that your friend, Charles, doesn't know this is a business arrangement. He thinks I'm your current girlfriend, is that correct?'

His grey eyes locked with hers.

'Yes. He's seen how, whenever I've asked girls to accompany me on such occasions, articles in the press about possible romance and wedding bells appear the following day. I'm so fed up with the press hounding me! I thought this would be a good solution. Charles would still be very surprised, though, to hear I paid someone to come with me, and I don't want to disillusion him. You just need to watch what you say, and try to keep the conversation as neutral as possible.'

Joanne looked down and played with

the clasp of her clutch bag. He had explained why he'd hired her for the evening, and she could understand. She didn't like his attitude, but she didn't need to.

'I'll do my best.'

Benedict was thankful to find she sounded amenable, and that she seemed to understand what was required of her. It would be disastrous if she pulled a long face all evening. There was something about Joanne that made him want to soften his usual, provocative style with strangers.

'Just out of interest, have you done this sort of thing often?'

Joanne avoided his face and looked over his shoulder at the mirror behind him. She reminded herself of Colleen's advice, that she should be more assertive, and she straightened her back. She reconsidered his face.

'No. As a matter of fact, this is the first time.'

'And why now?' His dark brows lifted.

'Because I'm unemployed, and I

need the money to pay my rent and buy food while I'm looking for a new job. I happened to spot the agency's advertisement, and I got in touch to enquire about the possibility of joining their books last week.'

He nodded. 'That's honest enough. Let's go then.'

He stuck his elbow out, and she tucked her arm through his, being careful not to entangle her wrap as she did so.

As they walked towards the lift, Benedict nodding occasionally towards people he knew, she said softly, 'I don't even know what this evening is about. Why are you here? Is there a special reason?'

Smiling at someone else they passed, his eyes flicked back to her, and he watched her face as he explained.

'It's to celebrate the final amalgamation of two of my companies into a more flexible and cost-efficient unit. Both were operating in similar fields, so I decided to cut administration costs without weakening the production aspect of things.'

He paused. 'I read in the information the agency sent me that you've a degree in economics, so I'm sure I don't need to explain. You can imagine what's involved in blending two companies.' His curiosity must have triumphed again, because he added. 'Out of interest, why on earth are you unemployed? You have a good degree. It shouldn't be a problem to find something suitable in London.'

Joanne was listening, while thinking about how amalgamating two companies would inevitably mean the loss of some people's jobs. She didn't think he'd understand why she'd lost her jobs. He was too far up in the executive hierarchy and wouldn't remember what went on in the lower levels of company management. He'd call the petty disputes, rivalries, and conflicts among people who were still climbing the ladder a waste of everyone's time. He would be right in one way, of course — but she'd been caught in the crossfire, and saw things differently. She hedged around the question and made a face.

'It's complicated. I just don't fit in.' Her usual, determined honesty emerged again, though. 'I'm hoping to find a job soon that I enjoy; one that matches my skills and ability.'

His brows lifted, and he viewed her for a second or two, but didn't reply as he guided them into the empty lift.

There was a mirror on the wall and Joanne had a good chance to view them as a pair. They looked good. His evening dress was clearly expensive, and he wore it like someone who was completely at ease with himself. His aftershave was pleasant, even if his proximity made her nervous. She was glad that her own appearance gave him no reason to be disappointed that he'd chosen her from the agency's list. She hoped the evening would proceed without any hiccoughs.

The lift rose silently up to the right level, and they exited and crossed the hallway leading directly into the ball-room. She was glad to disengage her arm when someone stopped him for a moment. Think positive, was her motto this evening. Confidence would get her through everything, if she relaxed and just did her best to follow his lead. He wasn't likely to dump her with a bunch of strangers for too long, in case she said the wrong thing.

The room was already full of people and chatter when they arrived. With Joanne hanging on his arm again, he guided them towards a man standing near one of the corners. He had a bundle of papers in his hands and clearly looked to be in charge of the evening's organization. Joanne couldn't fail to notice how people eyed them with careful deliberation as they passed. Benedict North was probably the boss of every person present. If not their direct boss, at least, they knew he was responsible for their income in some way. The men looked at him with hesitant respect and the women eyed Joanne with envy. She guessed that a lot of them were probably pricing her dress. She wondered what they'd think if they knew she was wearing borrowed feathers. Despite her efforts to remain cool, Joanne's nervousness grew, and she was now glad of the contact with his arm. It helped to keep her self-confidence alive as they moved along. She'd attended business dos in the past, but she'd never been at the centre of people's interest before.

The room was beautiful. It had fine, polished floors, huge chandeliers, and antique sideboards along the walls, displaying lavish flower arrangements in large porcelain containers. A number of large, round tables filled almost all the rest of the available space. They were covered with pristine, white tablecloths. They were already laid with shining cutlery and sparkling crystal, and small flower arrangements decorated their centres. A five-piece band on a raised podium was already playing music, and a space for dancing had been left free in front of the dais. At the moment, the hum of people's voices as they tried to find their allotted places drowned the orchestra's efforts.

Benedict stopped in front of the man

with the papers. 'Everything organized, Bob?'

The man nodded. Benedict indicated Joanne. 'This is Joanne Courtland.'

Bob gave her a brief glance. 'Pleased to meet you.' Returning his attention to Benedict, he continued, 'Anyone who should be here has already arrived. Your table is centre-front. I've scheduled your speech for roughly halfway through, and Walter Simonds is making a short one about how the amalgamation has gone smoothly, et cetera, just before that.'

'Right! See you later then.'

Benedict cupped her elbow in his hand once more, and guided them towards the assigned table in its prominent position. On the way, he said a few words of greeting to some people here and there. Joanne smiled, and tried to look at ease. When they reached their table, he pulled back her chair and waited for her to be seated. The other places were all occupied, and he introduced her briefly.

'This is Joanne Courtland. Joanne, this is Mr and Mrs Tony Smith — Tony's our financial director — and Mr and Mrs Ken Buchan. Ken is chief of personnel in the new company. Then, over here, we have Harry Green, and his wife Mary. Harry's one of our accountants. And this is Bob Watson, head of our research laboratories. The man at your side is Charles, our art advisor.'

They all murmured their greetings, and Joanne smiled at them in turn and said, 'Hello.'

The Master of Ceremonies welcomed everyone and made some opening preamble before the meal was served. Joanne was too nervous to eat much, but what she did manage tasted delicious. Benedict was on her right, and his friend, Charles, on her left. After a while, people's initial stiffness relaxed and they began to chat about work, about their families, and about recent holidays and other activities. Joanne tried to appear interested in everything, and Benedict gave her the chance to comment on remarks that he knew she could manage. She did so with carefully calculated answers.

After the meal, Walter Simonds rose to give a resume about what had taken place, then Benedict got up to give his speech. He spoke off-the-cuff. Even though Joanne had her reservations about him, and had decided he probably had quite a calculating personality, the way that he spoke about the amalgamation — the reasons, the negative and positive results, and the way people had reacted — impressed her. He certainly had his finger on the pulse of what was going on. She could tell by the expressions on people's faces that they knew he was in control. He assured them that the amalgamation was a necessity, for the survival of both companies in the long run, and for the benefit of all of the employees. He emphasized the efforts made to render the redundancies socially bearable by initiating early retirement in as many cases as possible, or giving others the chance of a job in another company. Resounding applause rewarded him at the end. He nodded to the bandleader and held out his hand towards her to open the dancing.

Joanne swallowed a huge lump in her throat as he led her onto the floor and began to dance. Joanne had never been more grateful that she'd taken dance lessons whilst at university. His steps were easy to follow, and she wondered when he'd found time to learn how to dance. They circled the empty dance floor together without any mishaps. She was intensely aware of their physical closeness, but kept her eyes on the front of his dinner jacket. After a couple of minutes, others joined them, and soon the floor was humming. Benedict led her back to their table and she drank a very welcome gulp of cold water. A few minutes later, Benedict asked one of the wives at their table for a dance, and he left her.

Joanne was sat watching the activities when Charles interrupted her observations.

'I'm not much of a dancer, but if you enjoy it and you don't mind me tramping all over your feet, we could give it a whirl?'

She turned and smiled at him. 'No need to make yourself miserable. I'm fine. I don't need to dance around all the time; in fact, I think I prefer to watch.'

He viewed her silently for a moment. 'You're very different to the kind of girlfriend Benedict usually brings. They're usually mad about dancing, and never stop talking. In fact, I can't remember him ever mentioning your name before now. Where did you two meet?'

Joanne didn't want to get into hot water. 'That's a long story! Ask Benedict about it one day.' Trying to divert him, she commented, 'He told me that you're one of his few real friends.'

'Yes, I probably am. He doesn't give his friendship easily, but we've shared bad times and good times together. He's always been there for me, and I think he knows I'm there for him too, whenever he needs me. His father made his life hell until he left home, and that has done a lot to make him who he is.' He looked at her. 'You know about Benedict's parents?'

She tried to sound nonchalant. 'Not in much detail. He only skimmed over family and the like.'

Charles pushed a strand of his fair hair back into place. 'His father's a vicar in Sussex, and he wanted Benedict to go into the church. Benedict rebelled, and since then, the two of them have only a modicum of contact. His mother has tried to keep things boiling, but his dad is a bit of an authoritarian. He just didn't want to accept that Benedict wasn't destined to end up in a country vicarage. He tried everything he could to dissuade Benedict from applying to the London School of Economics, and more or less forced Benedict to pay his own way when he went. Even though he could have helped, he didn't. Benedict had to fight every step of the way to get to where he is today. He's proved his father wrong. He's a born businessman. That isn't the whole story though. I expect he's mentioned his charitable organization?'

'No, he hasn't. What's that about?'

'A percentage of company profits, and of his own earnings, go to a company that bores wells and provides small solar panels for cooking and Internet connection in a couple of countries in Africa.'

'It sounds like a great idea.'

'It is. There have been lots of hiccoughs along the way, though. Once the wells are finished, they sometimes still need pumps, and that complicates the undertaking, because machines of any kind need maintenance, power, and spare parts. Last time we talked about it, he told me he's started training programmes to ensure the people on the spot can handle and maintain things.' Charles paused. 'His father might not appreciate what Benedict has achieved in the world of commercial business, but in his own way, Benedict has provided more tangible support for people who really need help, than his father has in all his years as a vicar.'

Hoping to seem sympathetic, she nodded. 'It must be difficult if you're at loggerheads with your parents. Mine supported me all the way. It was a big sacrifice for them to provide my university fees, but they did it anyway. I'll always be grateful for that.'

His pale brows lifted. 'You went to university? What did you study?'

'Economics and history.'

'By gad! At last, he's chosen someone with brains, as well as looks.'

She joined in with his laughter.

His eyes twinkled. 'I think I like you, Joanne Courtland. I can understand why Benedict does.'

'I'm glad that you do, Charles. I think I like you, too.'

Charles took a sip of red wine and leaned back into his chair. 'Do you know that Benedict has a terrible reputation as far as women go? He was very headstrong and uncaring, and never bothered about what anyone thought of him. In the early years, when he was still in the process of building his empire, there was a veritable parade of women in his life. I remember a vibrant French actress in particular, and another girl, who was allegedly an interior architect — I don't think she knew one end of a tape measure from the other, but that's what she claimed to be, anyway. Both of them lasted a bit longer than average, but they were the exceptions to the rule. There were quite a few in-between, and others since then. When I think about how he burned the candle at both ends to establish himself in the world of business, it's a mystery how he found the time. He worked day and night. He's calmed down a lot in the last couple of years, though, and lately, I even wondered if he was turning into a confirmed bachelor. Although all the mamas of eligible daughters he meets are still angling for his attention. Now that I've met you, I think they need to adjust their expectations. I can put some of them off the scent if I mention he has a serious girlfriend at last.'

Feeling a growing dismay, she said swiftly, 'Don't do that. It wouldn't be the truth. We don't know each other that well yet. We still have a very long way to go before anyone can pretend it's serious.'

She hoped that it sounded convincing, and that it was the right thing to say.

'I always thought he was far too intelligent to attach himself to an empty-headed girl. Someone like that would bore him to death in no time at all. You are a pleasant surprise. What do you honestly think of him?'

'Me?' Joanne pretended to consider. 'To be candid, I'm still making my mind up about him. I can imagine it's hard for anyone to judge him properly. Most successful people seem to have had a colourful past. Perhaps it's automatically part of their development. I won't comment on his business acumen, it's obvious. On the personal side of things, if he attracts the attentions of doting mamas or infatuated girls but ignores them, well, I suppose that can cause resentment and lead to rumour mongering. The past sometimes colours the present with half-truths. You need to know someone really well to judge. I don't know him well enough to do that — not yet.' Joanne hoped she sounded sincere. She didn't know Benedict properly, and never would.

Charles looked thoughtful and smiled. 'You're quite right. Everyone should judge on merit, not hearsay.'

'What about you? Do you have someone special in your life?'

His eyes clouded over for a moment. 'I did once, but she ended up with someone else, and I've never met anyone comparable since.'

'Don't give up. You have to believe there's someone out there just waiting for you to turn up with a masterpiece under your arm; or even someone who paints masterpieces themselves.'

He sighed. 'I think that is part of my problem. In my business I seldom meet 'ordinary' women any more. Only rich people can afford to buy the kind of pictures I have in my gallery. The girls who visit my gallery are generally spoiled, snobbish, self-centred, bad mannered, and discourteous. I have trouble being polite to most of them for longer than five minutes.'

Her eyes searched the dance floor

and found Benedict dancing with his partner. He seemed to be listening politely to her conversation. For a brief moment he looked towards her and their eyes met. A shiver ran down her spine. She shook herself. How silly. She was letting his reputation affect her reactions. Charles followed the direction of her eyes.

'A lot of people presume Benedict is a complicated character because he seems detached and aloof, but anyone who knows him better sees another Benedict. One who is sometimes unbelievably generous, one who cares, who enjoys life, and has a very original sense of humour. He somehow manages to maintain a wall around his personal life, because he's learned the hard way that many people just want to exploit him and his position.'

Joanne was grappling with a suitable comment, but she was saved when someone came to ask her to dance. She gave Charles a reassuring nod and followed the stranger onto the dance floor. While they circled the floor and made polite conversation, her mind was busy with Charles' information about Benedict. There was more to Benedict North than met the eye. It didn't make any difference to her role this evening, but it was interesting — even though she knew she wouldn't see him again after tonight.

Joanne danced with several other men from the company who probably wanted to impress Benedict in some way. She danced once more with Benedict, too. He didn't talk very much when they circled among the throng. She didn't mind, because her thoughts about him were confused. She mused that celebrities were people with strengths and weaknesses, like anyone else. There was no point in wasting too much time on him; they were ships passing in the night. She even relaxed enough to realize she was enjoying the evening. She felt comfortable with his firm hold in the small of her back, and she ignored the fact that he was disturbing her in a way she didn't quite understand. She put it down to a kind of fan adoration, as if she were suddenly dancing with a film star. He twirled her round now and then, and he seemed very pleased with himself. He was smiling as he led her back to their table.

He leaned towards her and murmured he intended to leave soon, long before the evening was finished. The smell of his aftershave was stronger when he was so close.

'They are all glad when the management disappear so they can let their hair down at last.'

Joanne looked at the crowded floor and smiled. She picked up her bag.

'If you're ready, so am I.'

He looked at her approvingly. Nodding goodbye softly to the others, who were making their own preparations, she turned to Charles.

'Night, Charles.'

'Night, my dear. I'm pleased to have met you. I'm off to the bar for a nightcap. I know Benedict won't be joining me this evening, but I actually approve, wholeheartedly. See you again soon, I hope?'

Benedict tucked his hand under her elbow, and she was saved from giving a suitable reply.

With the occasional nod and word here and there, they made their way back to the lift and down to the foyer. Someone cornered him for a moment and she used the chance to ask the doorman to get her a taxi.

Benedict joined her again, and she stood at a loss for a moment, looking at him and wondering what to say. She wasn't usually so guarded, but now, when they were on their own, her nervousness increased.

'How are you getting home? By car?'

She cleared her throat. 'No, I don't own one. I just asked the doorman to get me a taxi.' She held out her hand. 'Thank you, Mr North. It was an enjoyable evening, much nicer than I expected. Good luck with all your future challenges and achievements!'

He took her hand and held it a moment too long.

'After you've called me Benedict all

evening, I think you are entitled to continue using my Christian name now, don't you? I'll wait until you are safely inside the taxi.'

Flustered, she answered, 'There's no need. I'm sure the doorman will get me one as fast as he can. I'll wait here, inside in the warm, until it arrives.'

Unexpectedly, he gave her a lopsided smile that made her heart skip a beat.

'How would it look if I left you on your own? It would spoil the illusion we've created this evening if someone saw me slinking away to leave you waiting for a taxi on your own, wouldn't it? Thank you, by the way, for playing your role to perfection.'

She coloured. 'It wasn't difficult. And I'm quite sure you never slink away. I imagine you always withdraw with the utmost dignity.'

Benedict nodded and laughed quietly. 'I try!'

The doorman came across. He tipped his cap. 'Miss!'

Joanne was glad to escape. 'Thanks!

I'm coming.' She wrapped the stole tighter and headed towards the door. She was dismayed to find Benedict still at her heels. Outside, he overtook her to open the door of the taxi. Joanne stared at him stupidly, but she got in. The wind blew his dark hair into an untidy mess and he ran his fingers through it to bring it back into shape.

'Where to?'

Joanne gave the driver her address, and Benedict handed him a couple of notes from his inside pocket before he slammed the door and lifted his hand in a silent farewell. Joanne watched him as the taxi drew away from the curb, and she couldn't resist looking back at his dark, silent figure still standing on the pavement. Somehow she felt a little deflated, like Cinderella after the ball.

4

Next morning, Colleen phoned before Joanne had even got out of bed.

'What do you think about Benedict North, and how did it go?'

Searching for her slippers with her toes, Joanne wedged her phone between her head and her shoulder and went into her mini kitchen to fill the kettle. Her free hand pushed her hair out of her face.

'He is definitely a dominant and self-confident man. He's not handsome in the Hollywood sense of the word, but he's very attractive and has charisma. Perhaps the fact that he controls so many companies plays its part in that. It's a subconscious effect.' Grudgingly, she added, 'But even knowing that, I must admit he's an interesting personality.'

Colleen sighed quietly at the other

end of the phone. 'Will you see him again? It would be so romantic if it all ends up like Cinderella and the Prince.'

Joanne smiled. 'No. I didn't lose one of my shoes on the way out, so I don't expect to see him again, and he's not my Prince Charming. Oh, before I forget, thank Paul for the lift. When I get my money for the evening, I'll take you both out for a pizza.'

Sounding disappointed, Colleen said, 'We had a colossal row last night. I don't think I'll be seeing him again. He came around to pick me up after he left you at the hotel, we got into a silly disagreement, and one harsh word led to another.'

In the process of taking a piece of bread from the bag and popping it into the toaster, Joanne paused to say, 'I thought you two were serious?'

'Did you? No, we weren't, not really. I think he was just a habit I got into. I already noticed that he eyed other girls all the time. It annoyed me, but I tried to ignore it. We were talking about all kinds of things last night, and I just told him I didn't like him flirting around. He got ratty and told me I didn't own him, and all that crap, so I told him it was fine by me if we called it a day so that he's free to play the field again. I basically told him he could get lost. Being honest, I've known for a while that he was just someone who filled the gap at my side whenever I went out. I also know I won't miss him, and that's sad, in a way. I just wasted my time and his.'

'And you're not miserable? Be honest, Colleen!'

'No, cross my heart and hope to die! He wasn't important. I went out with him for the wrong reasons. Look, why don't you come round later on? There's a good film on the TV — a Scandinavian thriller. I'll buy some chocolate and a bottle of wine.'

'What time does it finish?'

'Round eleven, but if you're worried about going home late on the tube, you can always stay over.'

Joanne liked the idea. 'Okay. That sounds good. When I've had breakfast, I'm taking my dress back to the hire firm, because it's cheaper if I return it without delay. Then I need to go shopping. It'll be my treat to get us a bottle of red and a box of chocolates. I'll come round about six-thirty. That okay?'

'Fine. It's definitely a better idea than watching people getting tanked up in the pub. See you later. Oh! By the way, were there any reporters there last night? Will I see a photo of you on his arm in the newspapers tomorrow?'

'I didn't see anyone with a camera. Only invited people were taking photos with their phones. I'd hate to see my photo in the paper.'

* * *

After breakfast, she headed for the West End again, and carried the box with the dress down the street to the hire company. Joanne was disappointed to find Granville wasn't on duty. A middle-aged woman with a friendly face took the dress, checked it quickly and worked out the difference between Joanne's deposit, the charge, and what she was entitled to get back. Looking at it spread out on the counter, Joanne felt wistful. It was a beautiful dress.

★ ★ ★

A week later, she felt jubilant. In the course of the last couple of days, she'd been asked to go to interviews for two jobs, the first of which was for a job in a wholesale toy-trading business.

'Well, what do you think?' Mrs Prothero's husband had died quite recently. She was a tiny, delicate-looking, elderly lady, and the present owner of the company. She was faced with either selling the company, or finding a manager she could afford.

Joanne didn't know much about the manufacturing or selling of toys, but she could sort that out easily enough. There were two people working in the warehouse, Bill and Sally. They handled the arrival of the stock to the warehouse and its transport from the shelves to the retailers. She'd be responsible for all the paperwork and the rest. She'd need to grasp the rudiments of basic book-keeping pretty fast, but she understood the theory; she'd just never had to employ it. Joanne thought it would be great to have a job where she was responsible for everything, from beginning to end.

Joanne smiled confidently. 'I think it would be an interesting challenge, and I'd like to work here.'

Mrs Prothero smiled broadly. 'I'm glad you think so. I would hate to see Bill and Sally out of a job. They've both worked for us for more years than I care to remember, and I know just how much my husband would want me to keep things going.'

Joanne nodded. 'I understand. Do you know anything about how your husband organized the office work?'

The older woman shook her head vigorously. 'Not a thing! I went to the toy fairs with my hubby to help pick out new stock that we thought would sell, but apart from that, I had nothing to do with it at all. Bill and Sally know next to nothing about the office work either, so you'll be on your own. You'll just have to plough your way through it all until you've figured it out.' She paused. 'You're sure you don't mind working in a small firm like this? You won't meet many people in this job, you know. Most of our customers have been with us for years, and I think lots of them order everything by phone or via the computer these days.' She continued, 'I can't pretend that I like all the plastic stuff we sell, but the majority of people are not prepared to pay for wooden things, or the high quality toys we traded in years ago. Parents don't seem to mind that their kids end up sucking question-able colours and poisonous plastics these days. As long as it's brightly coloured and big enough, everyone is happy!'

Joanne laughed. 'No, I don't mind being on my own. Not at all.'

'And the wage? I expect you could earn a lot more in a bigger company.' The old lady's eyes widened expectantly, as if she anticipated bad news.

Joanne reassured her. 'Your offer is a fair one, considering the size of the company. I didn't reckon with more. And I won't come running to you for a pay rise every five minutes, either. I'll manage quite comfortably. I'm not someone who wants to replace my wardrobe every six months.'

'You'll be so isolated in this job, no one will notice if you don't replace it every six years! You're sure?'

Joanne nodded. She clearly needed to set her employer's mind at rest. 'Absolutely. I'm looking forward to it. I'll sort out what went on in the office, make an appointment with the bank manager, and check things through generally. When I have a good idea of how things stand, I can put you in the picture about future prospects, and we'll take things from there.'

Mrs Prothero held out her hand and

said, 'That sounds wonderful. We have a deal.'

Joanne didn't hesitate. She shook it.

'Come round to see me anytime you need. We can have a cup of tea and talk through how you're getting on. I live in the next street, at number twenty-three. It's the nineteen-twenties, red-bricked house on the corner. Well, I must be off. It's my bridge afternoon, and I don't want to be late.'

Joanne had to smother a smile. It was the first time she had ever heard of a boss who was happy to learn about her company's prospects over a cup of tea in her private sitting room. Joanne followed her out through a smaller, wooden door, set into the large warehouse double doors. They said goodbye to each other, and Joanne watched for a moment as the spritely figure strode off down the road. She hadn't asked Mrs Prothero if there had been other applicants. She was just glad she now had a job that she thought she'd enjoy doing.

She cancelled the other interview. It

was with the owner of a small building company. She knew even less about building materials and construction methods than she did toys. The workers would be out on building sites all day, so there was no one to ask. It was easy to explain she had another offer, for work that suited her qualifications better.

She telephoned Mrs Partridge at the agency and told her she'd found herself a job. Mrs Partridge wished her luck, and told her to get in touch again if things went wrong. Joanne was determined that wouldn't happen. There would be no mistrusting, competitive colleagues trying to trip her up. There was no excuse this time if things went wrong.

* * *

She started work at the wholesalers at the beginning of the following week. Her office was a cubbyhole, built into the roof's construction. It was chilly at this time of year, because it only had one electric radiator that was automatically

81

turned off every afternoon. Joanne soon learned to compensate with her second-best boots, thick sweaters and warm trousers. Her footsteps echoed through the high room whenever she clattered up or down the metal stairs.

She'd met Bill and Sally briefly when she came for the interview. They spent most of their working lives among the shelving system. They either needed to collect an item from its resting place for transporting elsewhere, or to store new arrivals in their appropriate temporary positions. Joanne guessed they were nervous, and wondering if she intended to change things. She could tell they were well organized, though, and decided not to interrupt them with pointless chitchat until they were used to her. She was naturally friendly by nature and they began to exchange generalities, and then more personal information, within a day or two. All three of them relaxed and soon felt happy with the new situation.

It didn't take her long to find out that, even if Mr Prothero was an elderly boss, he had an organized computer system, and an efficient filing system too. She'd visited the central library before she started, to get a better insight into wholesaling and what was involved. It had been time well spent, and had given her a rough idea what she had to do, and what was important. She used old contracts to determine the profit margin if someone asked for an estimate. Old customers rarely quibbled, and she soon got the hang of bargaining with anyone who did.

Phone calls were, generally, her only interruptions. Manufacturers rarely came personally, although Bill told her that a company representative might turn up with their newest catalogue, now and then. Mr Prothero always knew what had entered or left the warehouse because Bill input- ted arrivals and departures immediately into his computer. That meant Joanne could tell at a glance if they had what a customer wanted and what stock was still available. One or two customers asked why Mr Prothero wasn't handling things any more, and she had to explain. People sounded genuinely sorry when they heard he'd died. Joanne surmised that he must have been a nice person, as well as an efficient worker.

* * *

Joanne went downstairs with a faxed order in her hand to give to Bill in his cubbyhole, and in return, she received a bundle of new deliveries lists they'd received since her arrival.

'I've kept them up to date, but old Prothero always checked through them to see if I'd forgotten one. There's always the chance that could happen when I'm very busy. It would be a good idea if you carried on doing so. All the other ones I've handled since he died are upstairs on your desk.'

Joanne nodded and said, 'Yes, I saw them, thanks. Have you been here a long time, Bill?'

'Over ten years. Prothero did everything on his own until I joined him. He started out in his garage, and used his garden shed for storage until he was properly established. Then he bought this place.' He shuffled his feet, and nodded as he said, 'He was a good boss. Always fair, and always interested in Sally and me. If we had problems, he was the first one who was ready to help.'

'He sounds like a nice man. I hope I can rely on you for help, too, Bill. I bet you have a lot of inside knowledge about the customers. Which ones are slow payers, which firms help without quibbling in an emergency, that sort of thing. I'm still very apprehensive about buying new stock, because I know practically nothing about the world of toys. I'm hoping that you and Sally can help me there. I can manage the office work, but success or failure depends on us having the right toys on offer.'

Bill was impressed that she'd admitted her weaknesses straight off. His face took on a friendly look and his eyes twinkled.

'Mrs Prothero used to go with her

husband to toy fairs to buy stuff, and in the last couple of years, they used to take Sally along with them, too. It's almost as if he realized he needed to train someone else. Sally's good. She's been here for over five years, and she has a feeling about what will sell or not.'

'Then Sally is our long-term solution. Mrs Prothero isn't the youngest anymore, and she might not be able to go to fairs indefinitely. I'll talk to Sally about it. I'd like the company to carry on in the way Mr Prothero would have wanted it to. The only difference is that my wages have to come out of the profits now, in addition to what was needed before. Perhaps we'll have to find ways of increasing our turnover, but I'm sure if we work together, we can solve that problem, too.'

He nodded. 'You seem to have the right attitude, and we want to keep our jobs. This has always been a good firm to work for. Chat to Sally when you have a moment. Tell her what you told me, and I'm sure she'll be relieved that you intend to carry on in the same way Prothero did.' He looked at the sheet of paper she'd handed him. 'I'll get this order on the road by this afternoon.'

'Good. Christmas is not far off now. I expect it's the busiest time of the year?'

He grinned and shook his head. 'Most companies have already bought what they want and stocked up for Christmas. Shops have to work out what they want months in advance. The majority of them don't have any storage room these days, so once they've made their initial order they are forced thereafter to send for things day by day. That increases their delivery costs, but they don't want to disappoint customers, so they have to calculate properly. You'll find that a lot of the orders coming in now will be for Easter, or summer stuff, like beach balls for the holiday season.'

Joanne brushed her hair off her cheek. 'I can see I have a lot to learn, but with your help, and Sally's, I hope that we can continue to keep this business a going concern.'

The telephone in the office upstairs echoed through the open door. Joanne gave him a smile and darted back up the steps to answer it.

* * *

A few days later, with one eye still on some new stock entries she was working through, she rang Mrs Partridge's number. She'd just received her fee for the evening with Benedict.

Mrs Partridge answered straight away. 'The Partridge Agency. How can I help you?'

'Morning, Mrs Partridge. Joanne Courtland speaking. I wanted to thank you for the payment.'

'Oh! That's good of you to tell me it has arrived. I'm sorry I couldn't pay it straight away, but I expect you understand that sometimes these things do take a few days. I have to receive the payment from the client before I can pay you.'

'That's alright. I understand.'

'Is everything going well in your new job?'

'Yes, it is! I'm still finding my way around everything, but I'm very happy so far. It's just the kind of job and working atmosphere I wanted.'

'Good! Good! I'm so pleased it's all working out for you, although I was sorry to lose you from our lists. Mr North made an enquiry recently to ask if you could take on another engagement. He didn't want anyone else.'

Joanne stopped eyeing the computer and concentrated harder on the surface of the desk in front of her. Her voice was full of surprise. 'Really?'

'Yes. He even asked how he could contact you, but I explained that you did not work for us anymore, and even if you did, it was against our rules to give him any private information. From the tone of his voice, I think he was a bit put out. He told me point blank that it was a ridiculous prerequisite.'

Joanne laughed softly. 'I can imagine. He can afford to act like it's a foregone conclusion that he'll get what he wants. If I'd asked you about where he lived, or some such personal information, you wouldn't have told me either, would you?'

'No, and that's what I explained to him, but it didn't seem to satisfy him. He finished the conversation rather abruptly.'

Joanne laughed again. 'Ah well! I'm sorry if you've lost a customer, but you were right to stick to the rules. Thank you for the fee, Mrs Partridge. It is now bedded in my bank account and is helping to give my bank manager more confidence in my paying ability.'

Now it was Mrs Partridge's turn to laugh. 'I really am sorry to lose you. I think we would have got along fine. If you're ever . . .'

'I know. If I'm ever in a jam again, I'll phone you. Bye, Mrs P.'

'Bye, Joanne. Good luck!'

* * *

Joanne found she didn't mind if something had to be finished and it took extra working time — people often phoned at the last minute, even though they knew their business hours. She was gradually settling in and getting to grips with everything. Bill and Sally accepted her and they even lingered in the office for a chat and cup of coffee, when time allowed. Sally was a curly-headed, effervescent personality who knew precisely how to handle pushy or impatient deliverymen. Joanne kept out of their way, but she enjoyed listening to the laughter and flowery language that floated upstairs when Sally put somebody in their place.

Satisfied that she'd done all she could for the day, she put out the office light, clattered down the stairs, switched off the warehouse lighting, and locked the door. She didn't live far away and it was a pleasant, fresh, late afternoon. It was a relief to go home and feel secure in her job. She thought about what she had at home to make herself a meal. She lifted her shoulders, took a lungful of autumn air, and thanked the gods for a job she was determined to keep.

Turning into her street, she began to search in her bag for her keys. She wasn't aware of someone getting out of a big BMW parked on the opposite side of the road, until she was on the steps up to the doorway. She turned when she sensed there was someone behind her, and nearly bumped directly into Benedict North in her haste. As she was a few steps above him, they were face to face, so she was on a level with his grey eyes. The shock was written all over her face before she actually managed to find her voice.

'What are you doing here? How do you know where I live?' she squeaked.

His mouth curved upward. Now that the fright had faded, Joanne wished her heartbeat would calm itself. She felt flustered and caught out. He had no right to be here.

'I remembered most of the address you gave the taxi driver. I didn't know the exact number of your house — that agency woman wouldn't give it to me — so I parked in the street and waited.'

She swallowed a lump in her throat. As she looked at his craggy face and perfectly attired physique, her curiosity grew in leaps and bounds.

'And? Why are you waiting for me? You must already know that I no longer work for the agency. I've found myself a job.'

'Doing what?'

'I'm running the office of a small wholesaler.' She added quickly, 'Not that it's any of your business.'

He gave her a crooked smile. 'You're right. As a matter of fact, after that evening, I thought about offering you a job in one of my companies. I'm sure I can fit you in somewhere.'

Trying to sound assertive, she met his eyes and stated firmly, 'Thank you for being so benevolent, but that isn't necessary. I'm quite happy where I am.'

He nodded. 'Good. That isn't the reason I came, though. I want you to do me a favour.'

'A favour from me? I can't imagine why you might need my help in any way.'

'Charles is having a get-together at his country seat next weekend. You remember Charles, I hope? You seem to have made a big impression on him.'

She eyed him cautiously. 'Did I? I wasn't trying to impress anyone. And yes, I remember Charles. I liked him.'

'Well, he has been bending my ear ever since that evening because he wants to meet you again. He's been asking where we met, how long we've known each other — that sort of thing.' He watched her reaction. 'I even have the feeling he may have arranged this weekend purposely, just to be able to invite us along. That's why I'm here. I'd like you to come with me, if you have time.'

She drew in a deep breath. 'Benedict, I do not work for the agency anymore.'

He shuffled impatiently. 'I know that. I'm asking you for a favour. I don't want to disillusion Charles. I want him to believe I am still the upright, reliable chap he thinks I am.'

'Pardon?' she spluttered, and smothered a laugh. 'He told me about your past amorous escapades, so I think he has a very good idea of what you are like.'

'Did he now? That was unfair of him, especially when I wasn't around at the time to defend myself. Friends know too much about each other's strengths and weaknesses.'

'I think he also knew I wouldn't gossip, or divulge any tittle-tattle about your past to the wrong sources. That was part of the agency's agreement, wasn't it?'

Benedict gave her a smile that weakened her resistance, and increased her curiosity about him. The world in general only saw him as a cutthroat businessman. In contrast, his candid smile was surely more effective in winning someone's attention than any other crafty move. It suggested a sense of humour, and a softer side to his character, and she liked that. Joanne shook herself to concentrate on her answer.

'It's definitely not a good idea. An escapade like that could easily fall apart. Even if I agreed, we wouldn't be able to keep up the pretence for a whole weekend. I was glad to get through one evening without someone spotting it was all a performance. Anyway, why would I do you a favour? There's no reason why I should.'

'Agreed, but it would give Charles a lot of pleasure and help me out of a tight spot if you came. I would pay you, of course. The same rate as the agency.'

She stiffened noticeably. The colour faded from her face and she felt, and looked, shocked. Her eyes were stormy.

'My companionship is no longer a buyable commodity, Mr North. I thought you realized that.' She wished she'd never seen the agency's advertisement.

He ran his hand over his face and he looked repentant.

'That was crass of me. Please, accept my apologies. Look, my plan had been to convince Charles that we are on the brink of breaking up — but just recently, he's always in a rush when we speak, and it's not the kind of first sentence anyone employs, is it? He invited me — or rather us — for the weekend, and I thought it would give me plenty of opportunity to have a chat with him, without him rushing off somewhere, and convince him we're not love's young dream after all. It would only be this once. He has a lovely Georgian mansion in the depths of Sussex. He spends all his free time there. I'm sure you'd like it.' With a pleading tone to his voice, he tipped his head to one side and said, 'Friday night to Sunday lunchtime. A casual weekend; no dressing up or the like. Do it for Charles. Please!'

'I've only met both of you once! You're asking too much of me, Mr North. Invite some other woman, someone you know, and tell Charles you've swapped girlfriends. He told me you have plenty of socialites on your trail who would jump at the chance.'

'I used the agency's services that

evening precisely because I was fed up with doing just that. It's useless asking anyone else. Apart from anything, Charles knows most of the women I've been around with recently. For once, he was delighted in my choice of partner. It felt rather nice to have his approval. Joanne, you should know that I try never to ask anyone for a favour. It means I'm in debt to someone, and I don't like that. But for some strange reason, Charles has got a bee in his bonnet about you, and his friendship means a lot to me. I don't want to disillusion him by telling him the truth. Just a day or two together, and then I can pretend we've decided to call it a day.' He paused for a moment and Joanne could observe the way his skin stretched across his cheekbones and see how he had a slight dimple in his chin when he smiled. 'At least think about it overnight? I'll give you a call this time tomorrow. If you really feel you can't do it, I won't bother you again. Give me your number.'

Joanne studied him for a moment

and felt completely confused. It was such a strange situation, but she had to admit to herself that she was tempted. She pulled herself together and decided she needed time to think it through, properly, without the cool gaze of his grey eyes on her. It had an odd effect on her brain. Slowly, she nodded. She recited her number and he punched it quickly into his phone.

To her further consternation, he took her face between his hands. For a moment she thought he was going to kiss her, and she felt the heat stealing into her face. His nearness was disturbing and exciting at the same time. She froze on the spot.

'You are one of the most honest people I've met in quite a while. I'll respect your decision, but I'm hoping you'll agree.'

He released his hold. 'Please think about how pleased Charles will be if he can see us together again. I'm not sure why it's so important to him, but it is. I've known him for so long now, he almost means more to me than my own family.' He lifted his hand in a farewell gesture as he returned to his car, and called over his shoulder, 'I'll be in touch tomorrow evening.'

Joanne stood for a second, rooted to the spot. Then, without waiting for him to drive away, she turned and hurried up the steps into her flat. She wondered what he thought about the street and the house where she lived. He probably hadn't been this close to normal housing for years. When she was inside, she threw her keys onto the hall table and sat down with a thump in the middle of her Ikea couch.

She couldn't even ask Colleen for impartial advice. Colleen would just say, 'Go! Go! Go!' It still seemed strange to her that someone like Benedict North would want to bother with someone like her, even if he insisted it was just to please Charles. It seemed odd to her that he didn't want to disillusion Charles about a fake relationship, enough for him to waste an entire weekend with her, a stranger. He knew nothing about her, apart from the information from the agency. She could be a gold-digger, a shopaholic, a hypochondriac, a drunkard, a serial killer. She could have disgusting habits, or hate animals and children. On the other hand, she didn't know much about him either — apart from the fact that he was rich, that he controlled multiple companies, had a past history of women he'd left behind, and a problematic family.

She cradled her head between her hands for a moment and pondered her predicament. She'd just found a job she liked and her life was back on course again. Benedict North was a nuisance and an unsettling influence. She got up, took off her coat and started to boil water for spaghetti. Food was always a consolation. She pushed Benedict North and his suggestion aside and tried to concentrate on her dinner. She wasn't successful. Her musing haunted her for the rest of the evening, spoiling the television programme she tried to watch, and robbing her of enough concentration to read a book.

Next day, she concentrated on her job, but still didn't know what she was going to answer. A part of her wanted to spend time with him; another part told her it was a risky thing to do. She didn't fit his lifestyle. He was probably manipulating her in the same way he manipulated business competitors, just to get his own way. Her nervousness grew. By the time she got home, she still hadn't decided.

It was seven p.m., there had been no call, and Joanne had come to the conclusion that Benedict had decided it wasn't such a good idea after all. She felt a kind of relief — but also a little disappointment.

She jumped when her phone rang. It was Colleen.

'How are things? Coming on Saturday? Colin's bringing his latest girlfriend and we're all going to the Duck and Dog.'

'Yes, love to. Have you heard from Paul?'

'No, and I don't miss him. I'm so glad we finished. I don't think he'll turn up to be with our crowd again.'

Joanne laughed. 'I don't suppose he will. You brought him along in the first place. I've given up hope of ever meeting someone worth bringing along.'

'Never abandon hope! How's the job, okay?'

'Super. I've never felt better, and Bill and Sally are really nice people. I'm scheduled to go round to my boss on Wednesday to give her an idea of where we stand. I've spoken to the bank manager and the tax advisor, so I'll be able to give a decent account of myself.'

'Don't overdo it. You don't own the place. You just work there.'

'I know, I know. But it's so nice to feel good about my work for a change.'

Colleen laughed softly. 'I'm really pleased for you. Honestly! Must go, I've got something on the stove. See you Saturday. Come here first and we'll go together.'

'I will. Bye!'

Joanne realized she hadn't mentioned Benedict's request, but it didn't matter. They'd see each other at the weekend and she'd tell her then. Joanne had just settled down on the sofa when the phone rang again. What had Colleen forgotten to tell her this time?

She reached for the phone. 'Forgot something?'

'Pardon!'

'Oh.' She took a deep breath. 'Benedict. It's you. Sorry, I thought it was my friend. I thought she wanted to tell me something she'd forgotten.' Butterflies were swirling around in her stomach.

'I'm sorry for calling later than planned, but I just got back to my office. We had an important board meeting and it went on longer than I expected. Have you thought about it? Coming next weekend?'

'Do you mean the one in three days' time, or the next one after it?'

He sounded a bit impatient. 'The next weekend after this coming one.'

'Are there other people invited?'

'Yes, but not many. Charles doesn't like big crowds and fuss. Four or five, plus us, I would think. We all know one another.'

'I don't!'

'I can't change that. What do you say?'

Joanne threw caution to the wind; she'd like to see how the other half lived, and if she felt too uncomfortable, she could always call a taxi and get out.

'Yes. I'd like to see Charles again.'

There was a pregnant pause. 'Good. I wasn't sure you'd come. I wondered afterwards whether it wasn't just a mad idea after all.'

'I still think it's a mad idea, so if you want to forget it . . . ?'

'No, I don't.'

'One thing that does bother me is the clothes.'

'Clothes?'

'What should I wear? Perhaps you know how to dress for a 'relaxed' weekend in a country house in Sussex — I don't. I don't want to end up looking like a prize yokel.'

She heard him laugh softly. 'Good heavens! I've never given a thought to what people wear. It isn't important.'

'At least tell me what happens, so that I have an idea.'

'We eat, sleep, eat and sleep again!'

'What about between the meals? Do you go walking, play cards, watch TV, swim?'

'Walking, yes, but just the strolling kind, not hiking. Cards, perhaps. Swimming, no, TV is a possibility if everyone is feeling lazy. Charles loves a game of billiards. He has a stable with a couple of horses, so if you like riding . . . '

'I don't play billiards, and I can't ride!' said Joanne, sounding slightly panicked.

'Don't worry! Just the fact that you've come with me will be enough. If you take a book and choose a comfortable corner when other people get on your nerves, they'll think you're like me. Most people know I prefer a quiet life when I'm off duty. I usually avoid other people like the plague. Charles has a huge glasshouse, and growing orchids is one of his hobbies. He'll love you forever more if you ask to see them.'

'Right; so it's trousers, a skirt or two, pullovers, jacket, an anorak, sensible shoes, and a decent helping of serenity? Sounds like an interesting weekend.'

'Yes, I should think that's about right. I hope you won't get too bored. I really am grateful. I'll put Charles in the picture that we're not heading down the road to permanent happiness as soon as the chance arises. Then he will be satisfied that he tried to contribute to our everlasting relationship, but that it just didn't work out. And I'll never have to bother you again.'

'Hmm!'

'Got a pencil and paper? I'll give you my private number in case something crops up between then and now. Please don't ever pass it on, and please don't bother me with decisions about whether to wear black, brown, or orange. Quite honestly, I couldn't care less about your clothes.'

She scrabbled around for something

to write with. 'I'd like to remind you that any girlfriend of yours needs at least a little fashion sense. She wouldn't have caught your eye in the first place if she didn't. I'll do my best. Fire away with the number!'

He did. Joanne looked at scribbled figures. 'What time should I be ready?'

'Six-ish on Friday. Is that okay? I can't get away before then, but we'll have plenty of time to get to Charles' place for the evening meal. I'll pick you up.'

She took a breath and wiped her hand on her skirt. The man's expectation that everyone jumped when he called was impossible, but in a strange way she was looking forward to getting to know him better.

'Right. Until next Friday. Bye!' She pressed the disconnect button before he had a chance to reply.

5

Colleen had squealed when she heard about the invitation, and that Joanne had agreed to go.

'Remember every single detail. When you get back, I want to hear all about it.'

As the days passed and she thought about the weekend ahead, she felt more and more uncertain about what to wear. She needed moral support. After work one day, she went round to the hire company to look for Granville. She was delighted to find him there, and he smiled when she came in.

'Hi, beautiful. The dress came back when I wasn't here, but I presume the evening was a resounding success?'

'No one actually commented on the dress, or the person in it.'

'Ah! That's a good sign. If it didn't come up to scratch you would have heard various comments about it, usually nit-picking ones. The women were definitely jealous, that's why they didn't comment.' He rubbed his hands together. Today he had a dark suit with a velvet collar, and a white shirt with a stand-up collar and string tie, *a la* Karl Lagerfeld. 'What can I do for you today? Another evening date?'

Joanne explained about the weekend. 'I need your advice. You probably have more knowledge about countrified society than I do. My wardrobe is fairly run of the mill.'

He tilted his head and smiled. 'You like classical stuff, I can tell, and your things are perfectly okay. You have good taste, even if you are a bit conservative. When one doesn't have buckets of money to throw around, it is better to stick to classical stuff. From what you just told me, it really sounds like it will be a casual weekend. Trousers in plain colours; a skirt — tweed if possible; a Barbour jacket, because that's a must for any outdoor activities; some soft jumpers in pale colours; a stole, perhaps, for the evening in case it's chilly; flat shoes, a pair of high heels, and perhaps one nice dress, in case they do make a splash at the dinner table one evening. If one of the other females is kind-hearted, pump her for information about what's expected.'

'Okay, I have most of those items, but I don't have a Barbour jacket and I can't afford to buy one either. What if I bought a cheaper one, similar in style?'

He shook his head and uttered a soft tut-tut. 'Not done, I'm afraid. They'd spot that it wasn't a real Barbour straight away.' He studied her. 'We don't have any here, but my sister has one. I'll ask her to lend it to you for the weekend.'

Joanne's eyes widened. 'I can't borrow something from your sister! She doesn't know me.'

'She won't mind. Her wardrobe is bursting at the seams. Every time we do a clear out here, she gets first choice and you can imagine that she always chooses the best and most expensive items. She owes me. I wouldn't do it for just any customer, but I've taken a shine to you. Come around at the beginning of next week. I'm seeing her Saturday. A Barbour is a must if you're spending a weekend in the country!'

★   ★   ★

Joanne's brother, David, paid an unexpected visit while she was in the middle of packing. They caught up on each other's news and he made them tea while she was filling her holdall. Joanne had already hung out the things she intended to take with her, so it was merely a case of folding them and packing them.

'Where are you going?'

Joanne didn't want to explain about Benedict, or how she'd come to meet him. Intentionally or unintentionally, David was bound to tell her parents, and they would be shocked. Instead, she said, 'Someone I know invited me for the weekend. His name is Charles

112

Fitzherbert. A friend of his is picking me up.' She looked at her watch. 'Soon! Look, I'm sorry to throw you out like this, but I didn't reckon with you turning up today.'

David laughed, and ran his fingers through his sandy hair that had been turned almost blond from the summer sun. 'Don't worry about it. I had to come up to headquarters in London to clear something up anyway; I just dropped in on the off chance.' His hazel eyes twinkled. 'I'll catch an earlier train than I planned. When we've finished our tea, I'll be off. When are you next coming home? I'll arrange for Julie and me to come home, when you're there.'

'I'm not sure yet. I'll be phoning Mum next week as usual, perhaps we'll arrange something then.'

He nodded. 'Okay. I'll tell Julie to phone Mum and ask her to include us in the plans. You know how I hate phone calls. I spend half my life on the phone at work. I avoid it like the plague at home. Julie, on the other hand, seems to love chatting on it for hours.'

'It's a good thing she does, otherwise Mum wouldn't know if you were alive or dead.' She waited apprehensively and had to stop herself going to the window every other minute to see if he was there. 'They had a great holiday in Morocco.'

'So I gather!'

They both heard a car slowing down, and David crossed to the window. He looked out and whistled. 'Wow! That's the latest BMW, and with all the extras by the look of it. I must say, you are moving in illustrious circles these days!'

'Ready? I don't want to keep him waiting.'

'Yes, sure.' He took her cup and put it with his own in the sink. He donned his jacket and picked up her holdall.

She led the way down the steps, and when Benedict saw them, he got out and came to take her bag from David. He hesitated for a fraction of a second when he saw him. He turned to Joanne. 'Sorry, I'm late, aren't I?'

'No problem!' She turned towards her brother, who was still inspecting the BMW. 'This is David. David, this is Benedict.'

The two men nodded at each other.

David bent and kissed her cheek. 'I'll be off then. Take care and have a good time. See you soon, love! Bye, Benedict.'

'Yes, bye!'

Benedict opened the car door.

Lifting his hand in a casual farewell, David set off in the opposite direction.

Joanne got in and noticed raindrops were spotting the windscreen. She remembered David had brought an umbrella with him, and left without it.

'Oh bother. David has forgotten his umbrella again. He has a brain like a sieve sometimes. I bet he won't even remember where he's left it.'

She leaned back into the leather seat and made herself comfortable. Benedict made ready to pull out into the traffic, and it gave her time to steady her emotions. She fumbled in her bag for her phone and called David. 'David, you've forgotten your umbrella. It's in the hallstand. If you have time, go back and get it. Do you have your key with you?'

He answered, and she nodded. 'Good! See you soon.'

She looked across at Benedict. His expression was tight and he was silent for a moment. She wondered if he'd had a hard day, but then he seemed to relax again.

'Let's hope there's not too much traffic heading out of London this afternoon. It's quicker to use the motorway most of the way to get to Charles' place, but if there's a holdup somewhere along the route it can be nerve-wracking,' he said.

'I don't mind. It's the weekend and I'm curious to see Charles' country house. We have as much time as we need. Surely it's better to have me in tow in your car than having to attend a dreary conference in London?'

He chuckled and seemed years younger for a moment. 'Yes, you're right. I'm looking forward to it too.'

She left him to concentrate on guiding them through the worst of the late afternoon traffic. She listened to the radio music, and gazed out of the window at the passing scenery. After a while she decided to ask some questions.

'So, Charles asked you how we met? We need to tell the same story, otherwise he'll soon see it was all a performance.'

He looked across briefly and nodded. Daylight was fading fast as they left the circular road and proceeded down some country roads that had high hedges and were a lot quieter, but also very narrow in places.

'Yes, I had to invent something fast.'

'And?'

'I told him I tipped some coffee over you in a bistro, and after my vain attempts at an apology, we shared another cup together and started talking.'

'Hmm! Possible. Did he swallow it? Where was this bistro?'

'Suggest something.'

'Regent Street? There's a nice little bistro called The Golden Slipper. I've been there often.'

'Okay. The Golden Slipper it is.' He considered her briefly. 'I see what you mean — we have to get our stories straight, otherwise we'll trip up. Tell me a bit more about yourself. Where you went to university, where you're working now, something about your friends, hobbies — that sort of thing.'

She nodded. 'It's more complicated than just turning up at Charles' house, isn't it? You'll have to fill me in on a few things too, so that I sound like I have genuine insight into your private life.' Noticing the lift of his brows in the headlights of a passing car, she hurried to say. 'You don't need to tell me anything too personal, of course. We can always fall back on the excuse we haven't known each other very long; but we ought to know a little about each other, you have to agree with that?'

He nodded. 'Yes, you're right. You start.'

Joanne did. She told him what her parents did, where she'd been to school and university, about where she'd travelled, and her hobbies. Then he told her a bit about himself. Nothing too private, but a little more than she already knew from the Internet. Among other things, she heard that he liked sailing but didn't have much free time to enjoy it, that he liked to travel, played squash regularly, and didn't have any siblings.

Daylight had completely faded by the time they came off the main road into a side turning. Minutes later, they drove through gates framed by two impressively tall pillars crowned with mythical figures. They continued down a long drive, bordered by old trees. Some were evergreens, with their branches waving restlessly in the evening winds. Others were leafless, with skeleton branches that moved wildly back and forth in the gusty currents of air. The approach road was impressive, even though they swept up to the façade quickly.

Joanne looked through the windscreen and couldn't help saying, 'Gosh! What a wonderful place.'

The mansion, and its strategically placed greenery out front, was artificially illuminated and it had a feeling of altitude about it, because the house was built on a slight elevation. She tried to pick out details as they drew closer. She'd been to other Georgian mansions very often with Colleen, and she could tell it had excellent proportions and impressive symmetry. It was a typical Georgian mansion house with eight-paned windows. The house had gabled dormers high up in the roof and a flat-roof portico entranceway. As they drew up alongside some other cars, the double doors flew open and Charles came tumbling out. He must have heard them coming. The light from the entrance hall blazed down the shallow steps and spread across the pebbled driveway.

They sat silently for a second on their own and Joanne said, 'It is beautiful, isn't it?'

'Yes, it's been in Charles' family for several generations and Charles is fighting to keep it in top shape. I often spent school holidays here, with him and his father. The house and the adjoining estate was freedom for us both, in the best sense of the word.'

'I can imagine. As youngsters, if you had the run of the place, it must have been fantastic.'

'I think it may have planted the seeds of my ambition — I wanted to make enough money to be able to afford something like this. Funnily enough, when I did have enough money, I decided otherwise. You need more than just money to own a house like this. You need to be part of its history. Money can't buy that. Owning something that another family has had to desert isn't an achievement, it's a kind of takeover.'

'Hundreds of houses have changed hands through the centuries. Fortunes come and go. Families die out. It's surely better for a house to be properly maintained by someone new than to fall into decay and end up deserted because costs have got the upper hand. Then no one can restore it to its former glory, because it's too late.'

He chuckled. 'Perhaps you're right. Perhaps my personal connection to the house has coloured my attitude. Mansions cost the earth to maintain.'

Charles bounded towards the car and opened Joanne's door. He held out his hand to help her out.

'Hello, Joanne! Welcome! I'm really pleased you agreed to come.'

She placed her hand in his and got out as gracefully as she could.

'And I'm glad that you invited me.'

He kissed Joanne quickly on her cheek and said, 'Get the bags, Benedict, and follow us. The others are already here and we'll be having supper in an hour's time. When you've sorted your bags out, come down to the dining room.'

If Benedict minded acting as a porter, he didn't say so. She could tell that the two men were good friends. Benedict didn't blink an eye and moved to the car's boot.

Joanne went up the steps with Charles and through the entrance door into the hall. Facing her was a grand staircase, its sides bordered with intricate wrought-iron work. A flight of wide marble steps rose to a mid-level landing and then continued on symmetrically, to the left and the right, up to the second floor. The elegance of the Georgian Period was evident in the whole room — the muted colour of the elaborate plasterwork, the long eight-paned windows, and the niches around the hallway, housing classical statues. Her shoes echoed on the black and white marble floor for a few seconds before she paused to take another look around.

'What a beautiful room!'

Charles was right behind her; his words floated over her shoulder. 'Even if it is my home, I agree with you. It is, isn't it?

She turned to look up at him and said, truthfully, 'It is just about perfect. One of the nicest entrance halls I've ever seen!'

His smile emerged. 'The only thing that's not perfect in this whole house is its upkeep!'

Still admiring, she waited for Benedict to join them.

Charles said, 'I had to put you in the blue saloon this time, because I needed the others for the additional guests. It's the second door on the right. It has its own bathroom, so I hope that's a bit of a consolation. See you in half an hour or so.' He turned off to his left, and Joanne and Benedict started to climb the stairs.

Benedict was quiet, but he was never very talkative, so she didn't give it a second thought until they reached their designated room. Joanne had counted on them having two separate rooms, but they'd been allotted one. He opened the door and invited her to go inside with a sweep of his hand.

Feeling trepidation, she did so, and looked around. It was a beautiful room, with silk wallpaper, handsome furniture and long windows. It also had twin beds. The colour shot to her face and she swivelled to face him.

He lifted his shoulders and held the

palms of his hands upwards. 'I presumed we'd get adjoining rooms, so don't blame me. God knows this place has plenty of bedrooms.' He ran his hands through his hair. 'We'll have to make the best of it. Charles probably thought he was doing us a favour.' Trying to lessen her annoyance, he said, 'I hope you don't snore.'

She felt like stamping her foot. 'If I'd known about this, I would have told you to take a running jump.'

'Don't get in a tizzy! Do you think I like it? We are practically strangers, damn it!'

'It's your fault for not telling him the truth from the beginning. If you had, I wouldn't be here.' Her eyes were flashing.

'The situation was too complicated. I didn't want to admit I'd been dishonest with him. It's too late now. You surely don't expect me to go downstairs and demand that Charles gives us separate rooms. It's not just Charles waiting downstairs for us, there are a couple of other people I know too.'

'You are completely impossible, Benedict, do you know that?' She walked into the adjoining bathroom and slammed the door behind her. She sat down on the toilet lid. Was she prepared to go on with this farce? There was still time enough to walk out, find a hotel and return to London tomorrow by train.

He knocked on the door. 'Joanne, this is the twenty-first century. I had nothing to do with how Charles arranged the rooms. He didn't talk to me about it. He just presumed. You are very egotistical if you think I want to trick you into my bed. You're not my type; you're too sensitive, too conventional, and too critical. I can assure you, women queue up for my attention. Why should I go to the bother of tricking you into anything?'

Joanne realized she could say what she liked to him. There was nothing personal or emotional between them, and she could react without thinking twice about how he'd feel.

'You are an impossible and extremely conceited man. Do you ever think about the fact that the majority of women who chase you generally have their eyes on your bank account, and they don't give a damn about you as a person?'

He sounded more amused than surprised or dismayed.

'You're spot on with your observations. In fact, you're as sharp as a Swiss knife, but you don't shock me. I'm fully aware of what goes on. Now that you've tried to put me in my place, why don't you come out? I'm not in the habit of asking anyone for a favour, but I'll get the title of 'idiot of the year' among my friends if you don't help me get through this weekend. I promise, I won't touch you with a bargepole up here; I'll even give it to you in writing if you like.'

Joanne deliberated for a moment, but sounded less aggressive. 'I don't understand how you get awards for businessman of the year. You're not even astute enough to guess what your best friend will do when he invites you and your pretend girlfriend for the weekend. You've known Charles a long time, haven't you?'

There was a pause, and she wondered if he'd gone away, when he said, 'Yes. If you mean, do we talk about details like who sleeps where, and with whom, whenever we meet — why should we bother? I have better things to do and so does he. Charles has just presumed we are the epitome of a loving couple.'

Trying not to shout, Joanne said, 'It may be an unimportant detail for you or the kind of people you know, but I think it's an arrogant assumption of you and Charles to presume I want to sleep in the same room as you. What did you tell him about how long our relationship has been going on?'

She heard a faint splutter. 'Charles knows that the length of time I've been with someone wouldn't usually be a consideration.'

Digging her nails into the palms of her hands, she gritted her teeth. 'You may be surprised to know you can spend an enjoyable time with someone without having sex.'

'Can you? I can't say I've experienced much of that in the last couple of years.'

Seething, she reflected he was just proving he was another one of the arrogant, smug, and self-opinionated men she'd met in various businesses in the last couple of months. If anything, he was even worse, because he was also rich and powerful.

'Then I suggest it's time to change your priorities and treat women properly! Despite all your wealth and authority, your present attitude to women is appalling. You can't buy friendship and love — however much you might tell yourself you can.'

There was complete silence, and Joanne stared at the door for what seemed like an eternity.

Then he answered, in a brusque tone, 'The women I've known were in no doubt that I wasn't looking for anything more than a quick tumble between the sheets. There are plenty of women who want to grab my attention, even though they know that I am not looking for a permanent relationship. They still try to interest me in any way they can, including sex. I'm definitely not looking for love; it doesn't exist. Love is just another word for manipulating someone you know for your own purposes.' He paused. 'So what are you going to do? Are you leaving, or are you coming downstairs? Please rest assured, I have no underhand plans for sex with you, even if we do have to share the same room.'

Joanne was slightly shocked by their conversation. She'd never talked so spontaneously or told any other man what she thought about him in such honest terms. She didn't like his attitude and wanted him to know that. He was used to straight talking and wouldn't find it strange that she was shooting off her mouth like this. They came from two different worlds and had nothing in common — but that didn't mean she didn't need to be careful. He was still a very attractive and charismatic man. She was glad she'd been honest with him.

She also had to decide fast. She believed his assurances that he wouldn't touch her with a bargepole. Her main reason in coming with Benedict North was because she liked Charles, and she didn't want to disappoint him. Benedict wouldn't care about what she thought or said about him. Now that they'd cleared the air, he'd probably behave. She'd certainly made him dislike her — that's if he hadn't disliked her already.

'Okay! I'll stay. Give me five minutes to freshen up.' She opened the door. With heightened colour on her cheeks, she crossed the room without looking at him. She ruffled through her holdall for her cosmetic bag and returned to the bathroom.

6

Ten minutes later, she went down the wrought iron staircase at his side. He broke the silence.

'By the way, don't take any notice if I have to show you the occasional sign of affection. It's only for the benefit of the others. This is a game — I know that, and so do you.' He grabbed her hand and tucked it through his arm as he guided them towards a room on the right.

Joanne's throat was dry as she felt the closeness of his body and the possessive gesture of his arm linked with hers. He threw open the door with his free hand and they entered.

Charles was standing in front of an impressive marble fireplace with a roaring fire. He came towards them.

'I think most of you haven't had the pleasure of meeting Joanne? She seems to have tamed Benedict, and I can understand why. Joanne, this is Betty and William Attenborough. They live a couple of miles further down the road.'

A woman with brown hair, a wide face, and healthy colouring, stood up and gave Joanne a friendly look. 'I admit, I was curious to see Benedict's latest. Now I can understand why you caught his eye.'

Her husband hastened to smooth any wrong impression. 'Steady, old girl. This young lady isn't Benedict's latest business acquisition. She's flesh and blood.'

'I know that, Willy. It's about time that Benedict chose someone decent. I hope that he's been sensible for once.'

Joanne smiled at Betty and then laughed. 'I hope so too, but perhaps we all expect too much of Benedict.'

Betty's eyes twinkled, while Benedict's arm slipped to her waist and pulled her closer.

'I could argue on that point, but I won't.' Addressing Betty, he gave a crooked smile. 'There's no messing about with Joanne, believe me. That's why we get on so well.'

Joanne felt breathless from the feel of his hand and hoped it didn't show in her face. Charles introduced the others. 'This is Vanessa Curry. She's an old friend of both Benedict and me.'

Vanessa was elegant, in her early thirties, with a smile that didn't quite reach her eyes. Her clothes were designer items, even though they were completely casual in style. The muted colours suited her blond hair and blue eyes. From her expression, Joanne could tell she wasn't interested in welcoming a stranger, especially one she knew nothing about. She nodded and lifted her cocktail glass in Joanne's direction in greeting, and said, 'Less of the 'old', Charles, if you please.'

Charles laughed and proceeded to introduce the others. John and Lyn Leroy gave Benedict and Joanne a welcoming smile, and then Keith Pritchard, Ken Arber, and Millie Smith greeted them politely too. Everyone knew one another, with the exception of Joanne. For a couple of minutes, Joanne felt like a specimen under the lens of a magnifying glass, and she noted that there were nearly double the number of people here than Benedict had given her to believe there would be. Charles offered them a drink and Benedict unlinked his arm to accept his whiskey. Joanne took her sherry and was glad to have something to occupy her hands.

The conversation circled around events and people foreign to her, so Joanne let her thoughts wander. She examined the room more closely. She admired its proportions, the long windows looking out into the darkness and the oil paintings decorating the walls. The room was probably one that was well used. The sofas and easy chairs were covered in a green silk that was still beautiful, even though it was beginning to show its age. This house and this room immediately made her think of Colleen. Colleen's interest in antiques, paintings, furniture, buildings, and history in general, went back to their schooldays. Colleen would love this house. She still went to see every art exhibition, display, presentation or historical show that she possibly could. She was fascinated by the past, and Joanne often wondered where her interest came from. She'd studied economics, like Joanne, but she was still passionate about history. She often persuaded Joanne to go with her on her various outings, and Joanne was always surprised how much real knowledge Colleen had amassed about furniture, paintings, architectural styles and history in general. She had more books about history than anyone else Joanne knew.

While Charles' visitors continued to talk together in hushed groups, Charles came to stand next to her.

'This is a bit boring for you. You won't have a clue about what we're talking about.'

Joanne smiled at him. 'I don't mind. You all know each other very well and it's perfectly natural that you want to catch up on all the news. I was using the time to admire this room and the whole house.

I just thought how my friend, Colleen, would be over the moon to see it all. She loves history, and she continually drags me to see every exhibition and country mansion within travelling distance of London. Some houses are open throughout the year. Others are open for one single weekend in the whole year. She has to see them all. I'm interested too, and I enjoy going with her, but Colleen is exceedingly well informed about the historical and architectural side of things. I'm often gobsmacked by the knowledge and interest she shows.'

'If she's as young as you, that's pretty unusual, especially if she hasn't lived in that kind of background from childhood.'

'You mean belonging to the landed gentry and having a family history going back generations? No. I don't know where she gets her interest in history from; she's had it as long as I've known her.'

'What does she do?'

'She's an accountant in a tax advisor's office.'

137

'That's quite a mixture. Modern taxation problems in her working life, and history and historical buildings in her spare time.'

Joanne nodded. 'Personally, I think she should have taken up something to do with history professionally. She's good at her job, but her heart's not in it.'

'If she is ever hereabouts in the vicinity, tell her she's welcome to call. I'm not here all the time, but I am most weekends. I enjoy showing people around my modest abode. I have no plans to open it to the public at present, but it is an interesting place. Even I think it is a beautiful building.'

'Your home is quite special and I love it.'

From across the room, Benedict turned, giving Joanne a brief view of his profile. He was smiling, and for a second he took her breath away. Her knees went weak and she realized how much his appearance affected her. She wished it didn't. Under the circumstances, it was idiotic to admire someone like him. Benedict looked across at her chatting to Charles, with an expression that was partly derisive and partly amused. She looked away quickly and played with the stem of her glass. When she looked at him again, Vanessa had captured his attention. She listened to Charles talking about the house, while viewing Vanessa and Benedict together. It was clear that they got on well. Joanne straightened her pale yellow cashmere pullover and pushed one hand into the pocket of her fawn trousers. She felt quite satisfied with her appearance, even if Vanessa outshone every other woman in the room with her flowing silk blouse and figure-hugging pencil skirt. Betty was wearing a tweed skirt with a paisley blouse, Lyn wore a two-piece in pink jersey, and Millie had on a black dress that was a mite too tight.

Vanessa tilted her head to the side and looked up cajolingly at Benedict. She laughed at whatever he said, and did it too often. Joanne wondered if it was honest friendship, or if she was just trying to make the right impression. It was hard to tell if Benedict was enjoying their conversation or not. Joanne wondered if they were linked by mere friendship or something more. He had the gift of hiding behind an inscrutable mask while remaining outwardly friendly. If the two of them had known each other a long time, they must have a lot of similar interests and pursuits. Joanne couldn't imagine him wasting time on someone he didn't appreciate. She didn't like the idea of them together and dragged her attention away to concentrate on Charles again.

Soon after, the housekeeper announced the evening meal was ready, and they all followed Charles into an adjoining room, where a large, oval, cherry-wood table had been beautifully set to accommodate them all. Charles indicated where they should all sit. Joanne admired the Victorian silver, shining crystal and precious chinaware. She was looking forward to the meal; she was hungry and she guessed — rightly — that it would be to a very high standard.

The conversation flowed; mostly around local happenings and acquaintances, which Joanne knew nothing about. She didn't mind. As long as the others were busy among themselves, there was less likelihood of her putting her foot in it and making a mess of the evening for Benedict.

After the meal ended, they all returned to the sitting room and claimed various sofas, chairs and other seats. Someone suggested a game of cards and a four-some was quickly formed. The others remained chatting idly and listening to the comments from the card table.

Vanessa interrupted Joanne's mus-ings. 'Benedict tells me you went to university?'

'Yes, and I enjoyed it.'

'And what are you doing now?'

Linking her hands behind her back, she replied. 'I help run a toy ware-house.'

'Really? And you need to have a university degree to do that?'

'No, probably not, but it has helped

me have a wider understanding of how a business works.'

Vanessa turned to Benedict. 'Why didn't you find her a job in one of your businesses?'

Joanne objected to being addressed as 'her'. Vanessa knew her name.

Benedict swirled his whiskey around in his glass and looked at Joanne.

'Because she refused, and almost floored me by saying she didn't want to get involved with me outside our personal relationship. Not many people refuse an easy hoist up these days.'

It sounded like a true statement; but she realized it was a secret assessment of what he thought she was like. It was a hidden compliment.

Joanne met his eye and addressed Vanessa.

'Business and pleasure should never mix. I don't think I could ever work for Benedict. He's too demanding.' She wanted to shift the direction of the conversation. 'You've known each other a long time?'

Vanessa nodded. 'Yes, a long, long time. I met Charles and Benedict at a house party in Biarritz several years ago and we hit it off from the word go. It turned out that Benedict was a business acquaintance of my father, and Charles sold my sister some paintings prior to that, so we were already connected. Sometimes it's a small world, isn't it?'

'Yes, it is.' Joanne didn't think a fleeting meeting at a house party sounded like the foundations for a real friendship, but on the other hand a friendship had to start somewhere. It looked like they had wanted to keep in touch later — otherwise they wouldn't be here now. It also showed her that social rank still determined the degree of friendship. Outsiders were probably not welcome. She nodded politely. It didn't really matter.

Vanessa was still talking to her. 'What does your family do?'

'My parents are retired. My father used to be a teacher and my mother worked part-time for an estate agent.'

Vanessa said with raised eyebrows, 'Oh, I see. How unusual.'

Joanne could feel her hackles rising because of Vanessa's obvious snobbishness. She had to remind herself that she only needed to put up with it for two days. There was no point in trying to provoke Vanessa. She didn't need to enjoy her company. She looked at her watch and put her half-finished drink down on a nearby table.

'If you'll excuse me, I've had a busy week and I'm tired. I think I'll go to bed. I'm sure you and Benedict have loads to talk about.'

Vanessa touched his arm. 'Yes, we do. We don't see each other often enough these days, do we, Benedict?'

He didn't answer. Joanne caught Charles's eye at the card table and pointed upwards with a finger. He nodded, and turned back to the game.

Benedict said, 'Yes, go ahead. I'll join you in a couple of minutes. We're both tired — but not too tired, I hope?'

Joanne stared at him and felt the

colour flooding her cheeks. She turned away quickly, and left without another word. Upstairs in their room, she hurried to get ready for the night. Her flannel pyjamas decorated with tiny panda bears were hardly stylish or sexy. When she'd packed, she calculated that the rooms in an old house might be cold, and also that she'd be on her own. She got into bed and tucked the duvet tightly around her. The other twin bed was just an arm's length away. She looked at the shadows playing on the ceiling and willed herself to fall asleep before Benedict arrived.

To her surprise, and his, she was sleeping when he did. One of her legs had escaped the duvet and stuck out at an angle. He studied her sleeping features and noticed the panda bears. He smiled unconsciously; he couldn't remember when he had last spent a night in the same room with a woman who was as wholly disinterested in him as Joanne was.

Next morning, Joanne woke to feel weak beams of morning sunshine tickling her face. She sat up slowly and stretched. It took less than a fraction of a second for her brain to kick in and remember where she was, and why she was here. She stared at the other empty twin bed. The duvet was thrown back and the pillow dented. The room was silent and the door to the bathroom was wide open, so she was alone. She got out of bed gingerly and toddled to the window. Their room overlooked the land at the back of the house. The countryside was still under a veil of grey morning mist. Closer to the house, the fields and meadows were more visible and the area was well cared for. Her gaze drifted to the pebbled area directly below the window. Charles was talking to Benedict. He must have noticed the curtains moving and he looked up. She stepped back quickly, but not before she noticed his amused expression. She was annoyed with herself for reacting like a frightened mouse.

She hurried to shower, and dressed in narrow, beige trousers and an expensive caramel-coloured sweater that she'd bought in more prosperous times. She went down the impressive stairway and into the dining room. Betty was the only other one there.

She looked up.

'Oh, good morning. I thought I was the last one.'

Joanne looked briefly at her watch. 'It's not that late, is it? Normally I'm just about to set out for work at this time of day, so I'm not much later than usual.'

'I am. I'm an early starter. I'm busy in our stables by seven at the latest, every day. Slept late this morning. Too much alcohol last night, I expect. Everyone else seems to have disappeared or are already outside.' She waved her hand towards the sideboard where various dishes and silver-lidded containers were spread across the polished surface. 'Help yourself. I did. No one else seems to be around. Is Benedict up? Coffee is in the vacuum jugs.'

Joanne went towards the sideboard and nodded. 'He's out. With Charles.'

Betty nodded. 'He's usually an early starter too. I think they're planning a ride this morning. Coming?'

'I can't ride. I expect I'll go for a walk if I get bored.'

Biting the corner off a piece of toast Betty said, 'Pity. You should learn. Benedict couldn't ride when we first met, but he's a very competent rider these days.'

'I presume that once he's made up his mind to do something, he always does it well. I don't mind horses, as long as they're at a civilized distance. Their sheer size frightens me. I had a friend once who loved riding. She passed all the various tests and was always taking part in competitions. She spent all her spare time looking after her horse. If I went with her to the stables, her horse always used to try to nip me. I think it knew that I was frightened.'

'It did. Horses are intelligent and they like to have fun. If you haven't grown up with them or learned how to love them to bits, and are wary of them, they sense it. Vanessa grew up with them. She has no fears and is an impressive rider. Her parents have a grand house and magnificent stables. They breed hunters. I think she was the one who persuaded Benedict to have a go.'

Joanne shrugged. 'I'm not surprised. I can just imagine how she enjoys following the hounds.' She didn't intend to sound derisive, but that's how it came out.

Betty viewed her in silence for a moment. 'You're not the usual type of girl Benedict has in tow, are you?'

Joanne laughed softly. 'No, I expect I'm not. But then, why shouldn't Benedict and I be very different? Perhaps opposites do attract. I'm just a small-time manager. I'm small fry in comparison to what Benedict stands for. I'm not even sure I actually deserve the title of manager; perhaps office organizer would be more accurate. I think we even see life from two different viewpoints most of the time. Do you think that's a bad thing?' Joanne picked up some toast and joined Betty at the table.

Betty's eyes twinkled and she smiled at her. 'No, probably not. I've seen him with too many women who were after his money and his social standing, and didn't have a pennyworth of brains in their heads. I'd hate to see him end up with the wrong woman — although it's none of my business, and Willy continually tells me to keep my nose out of it. I like Benedict because he's an honest bloke, and there aren't many of those around these days. Apparently, he's honest but inflexible in his business dealings — but that's why he's so successful. Outwardly, he seldom lets human aspects triumph over his logic. That's a pity. I only know he is loyal to his friends and more generous than a lot of people imagine.'

'You can't run a business the size of the one he's built up unless you are prepared to be hard-nosed. You have to make unpopular decisions and rulings all the time. You also need to be extremely clever. Benedict is, and I don't suppose he wastes much time worrying about the long-term effect of his plans and decisions, or what other people think about him. He can't afford to do that,' said Joanne, matter-of-factly.

'You sound almost cynical about your boyfriend. I've known him for a long time and I'm sure he does think about the people he likes and how to secure long-term jobs for his employees. He's not God, and sometimes things don't work out, but I'm sure he does his best. If he makes an unpopular decision or says something unexpected, it doesn't mean he didn't think about the conse-quences. I do wish he had more happiness in his personal life; but perhaps you'll change that. There's no point amassing money, getting richer and richer, unless one day you ask what it's all for.'

'There are a lot of extremely rich people who never give a second thought as to why the majority of ordinary people struggle to earn enough to live just above the breadline. They probably think workers at the bottom of the ladder are stupid for being satisfied with what they have. That's the real difference: ambitious people are never satisfied.'

Betty laughed and got up. 'With your attitude, you must like Benedict an awful lot, and he you. You seem like two opposites. Still, I think it's a sign of the real thing, if you love someone despite their faults, and can accept them for who they are.'

Joanne looked down and buttered a piece of toast with exaggerated care. 'You're probably right,' she said. 'That's why a lot of marriages break down. Too many people try to change their chosen partner.'

Betty put her serviette next to her plate. 'Know what? I like you. Look at Willy and me. We're like chalk and cheese. I'm a horse fanatic and Willy has a hothouse full of exotic cacti. He's a well-respected, solid solicitor, and people think I'm dotty. But at the end of the day, we shut the door on the rest of the world and still enjoy being together. That's what counts. He hasn't tried to change me, and I don't want to change him. Right, I'm off — it's a damned shame you don't ride, I think Charles has planned a good jaunt for us this morning. We're riding over to Netherhold.'

'Enjoy yourself!'

'I will. Willy is in the library reading some dusty volume he discovered on one of the shelves. If you get bored, join him. He's very polite and would drop it to chat to you straight away. I'll tell Benedict I've seen you having breakfast. See you later.'

She strode off towards the door and disappeared quickly.

Joanne leaned back in her chair and reached for one of the newspapers from a pile that had been conveniently left on the side. Benedict would be gone for a couple of hours, and that meant she was free to do what she liked. The weekend looked like it would be less complicated than she expected. It was easy to chat to Betty. Perhaps the others were okay too. She'd have to play it by ear.

A quick glance out of the window told her that the morning mist was lifting. The sun was already highlighting the gold and russet colours of the ancient trees in the distance. She looked forward to going for a walk. She never had much chance to go for a proper walk, or be anywhere on her own in the town anymore. A quick glance through the newspaper and several cups of coffee put her in the right frame of mind to fetch her borrowed jacket and set out to cross the fields and climb one of the gentle hills at a distance from the house. She sat down on a layer of dry needles surrounding the base of an old fir tree and looked back towards Charles' house. There was a village in the distance, and among the undulating countryside she could see the roofs of isolated cottages or farmhouses. It was a delightful spot, and she breathed the sharp, clear morning air.

She'd shoved a book into her pocket at the last minute before she set out, and now she sighed contentedly as she retrieved it and searched for the right page. Leaning back against the trunk of the tree, she was cut off from the winds and she felt warm enough to remain reading for a while. Presently, though, she grew aware she'd been there too long and she was cold. It was time to go back to the house and see if the others had returned. She glanced towards the house and noticed a bunch of riders nearing the stables. They were back. She looked at her watch and was surprised at how quickly time had passed. She closed her book and made ready to get up and set off again.

Benedict came through the trees. His sudden appearance set her pulse racing and the effect shocked her for a second. She had to admit how elegant he looked in his riding attire.

'Where did you come from?'

'We got back a few minutes ago.'

'Yes, I saw everyone arriving. How did you get up here so fast?' She felt slightly flustered and her mouth was dry.

'I saw your scarf blowing in the wind when we were coming in. Betty told me you intended to go for a walk, and I knew no one else but you would be so foolhardy to stay out in the wind on this hill. I gave her my horse when we rounded the bend in the river, and came across the fields. I thought I should act like a besotted lover for a few minutes.' He held out his hand to help her up, and she had little choice but to take it.

Once standing, she disentangled their hands to brush the seat of her trousers.

'It wasn't very cold. I sat in the shelter of the tree. I haven't been here that long. I've only managed a couple of chapters and I was just on my way back because I was starting to feel cold.'

'Your hand is like a block of ice.'

'Is it? I always have cold hands.'

He stood and tapped his whip in his hand. 'How do you feel about the week-end so far? I gather that you had a chat with Betty this morning. She's taken a shine to you, and that doesn't happen very often.'

Meeting his glance and smoothing some stray strands of hair out of her face at the same time, she said, 'I like her too. She's a very honest person. I don't usually like that kind of horsey, gymkhana, village fair, country lady type of woman, especially when they don't work for a living, but somehow I couldn't help it. I think she was a bit surprised because I told her how different our attitudes are. I expect she's still wondering what you see in me.' She laughed and her green eyes twinkled.

He smiled. 'I'm sure she is. She's used to seeing me with compliant companions, not someone who's so sassy. I quite enjoy the fact that I've surprised them. I expect they thought you'd be like the rest. Charles knew you, but I think even Charles wanted confirmation that I was serious.'

'I like Charles and I don't like deceiving him. He's a gentleman, and this place is lovely.' She started to stroll back down the slope and he fell into step beside her. 'Where did you meet him?'

'School. I've known Charles longer than anyone else, apart from my parents. I went away to boarding school when I was eight, and Charles was already there. We clubbed together against the rest of the world. His mother died when he was quite young and he needed as much support as I did in an alien world.'

'Gosh! I can't imagine how hard it must be to be sent away at that age. I expect it's easy to believe your parents just want to get rid of you.'

He stared ahead of him, and said, without any emotional tone, 'Some of the kids were younger than that. It wasn't much fun, but my father had gone to the same prep school and he thought it was the best thing for me too. The fees must have crippled them at the time, but they were determined;

or rather, he was determined.'

'I gather you didn't like it. Wasn't it the best thing for you?' He helped her over a stile in the hedge.

He thought for a moment. 'Who knows if it was or not? I do know that I hated it. My friendship with Charles made it bearable. Most of the others came from old, established families, and I was an outsider. I suppose it formed me in a way. It made me more determined to outrun them all, and I have.' He suddenly realized he was giving away too much of himself and started walking again.

Joanne had to hurry to catch up with him. For the first time she felt real sympathy for him. He hadn't had a happy childhood and it had left him with festering wounds. No wonder he'd put all his energies into building up his empire. It was his way of proving his own worth. Her breath evaporated in the air and she had to rush to join him.

He noticed. 'Sorry!' He waited for a moment. Looking at her, he said,

'There's something about you that makes me tell you things I've never told other people.'

She grinned. 'Don't worry, I won't sell it to the News of the World; not unless you do something that shatters all my hopes and dreams.'

'Do you have any? Hopes and dreams?' He reached out to her face and tidied some escaping strands of hair.

Joanne swallowed hard and met his glance. 'Of course! We all have hopes and dreams, don't we?'

He shrugged. 'I'm not sure about that. Hang on to yours if you have any.' He looked towards the house. 'Oh, look, there's Betty waving to us.' He crushed her to him and he was so close it seemed natural that his mouth met hers.

She enjoyed the feeling of his warm lips. It was more exciting than she'd ever experienced before, and it sent shivers of desire racing through her. Her eyes widened with astonishment and they stared at each other wordlessly for a moment. Finally, he held her from him. Holding her arms, he explained, 'I was just showing Betty how much we're in love.' He turned to the figure standing on the terrace and waved. Betty waved back.

Joanne was still stupid with surprise, even though she knew his kiss was meaningless. She hadn't reckoned with the effect it was having on her, though. He brought her back to earth.

'Come on, if we don't hurry, the others will have finished lunch before we get back. I'm hungry!' He smiled. 'Betty is probably telling them that we've been dilly-dallying in the fields.'

She managed enough composure to say. 'In this weather, I doubt if anyone would be that stupid.'

★ ★ ★

The rest of the weekend passed happily. Joanne tried to avoid Vanessa as much as she could. They both had a masked aversion to each other. Joanne didn't like her snobbish, overbearing attitude, and Vanessa clearly didn't like the fact that she was Benedict's girlfriend.

After lunch, they all split up for a while. She followed Benedict upstairs to their room. He said he needed to contact his assistant and started searching through things. She decided to phone David.

'Hi! Everything okay? Did you go back for your umbrella? And did you lock the door?'

'Yes, and of course!'

Joanne saw Benedict's expression, and decided he must need peace to do whatever he wanted to do. She shortened her conversation. 'Right! I just wanted to be certain, love. Take care!'

She found her book and left him without another word. She went down to the library. Betty and Willy had gone for a nap. Vanessa was out in the stables, and the others had settled down to read the newspapers. Joanne enjoyed the seclusion and calm of the library. She skipped tea, and had a leisurely bath, before getting ready to meet the others for the evening meal.

She was glad she'd included a dress in her luggage. The colour flattered her hair and eyes, and gave her skin an attractive translucency. For some reason, she was pleased when she noted the glimpse of approval in Benedict's eyes as she joined him.

After dinner, they split up into groups, playing scrabble, watching TV, playing cards or wandering from group to group to chat. The fresh air was having its effect, and when Benedict and Charles suggested going down the local pub, she decided against joining them, as did Millie and Betty. Vanessa, the Leroys, Willy, Keith and Ken went off to get their coats to join them.

★　★　★

After a drawn-out breakfast next morning, and a brisk walk to the nearby river and back, everyone began to think about leaving. Benedict said he had to be back in time to catch an evening flight to Paris, and Joanne was happy to fall in with his plans. She packed quickly and noticed he'd already packed after getting up. They said goodbye to the others and Vanessa even managed to give her a cool farewell smile.

Charles pecked her cheek. 'I hope to see you again soon, and tell your friend she is welcome to take a look around the place anytime she likes.'

She smiled warmly. 'Thank you so much for a lovely weekend Charles. I enjoyed it. I'll tell Colleen, I'm sure she'll be interested.'

He nodded and after he followed them outside he turned to Benedict. 'See you soon. Give me a ring when you have time.'

Benedict nodded and loaded their bags into the boot. They set off, ploughing deep grooves into the pebbled surface. Joanne half-turned in her seat when they reached a slight bend, to wave to Charles still standing on the steps.

7

A few minutes later they were miles away from the house, and Benedict broke the silence.

'Was it too bad?'

Surprised that he had asked, she tilted her head to the side.

'No. In fact, it was a lot nicer than I expected.'

'Good, I'm glad. Thank you for coming with me. I hope that we've now satisfied Charles' curiosity. I still need a very good excuse about how we broke up for next time I see Charles. I was never with him long enough to even suggest things were not harmonious between us, but I'll invent something feasible, I promise!'

She ran her fingers through her hair. 'Easy. You could tell him we had a humdinger about money; you thought I was double-crossing you with a romantic Spaniard; you thought that I was planning to sell the story of our relationship to the gutter press. Tell him you caught me emptying your wallet, or bitching about you to my best friend and telling lies.'

He laughed and the white of his teeth flashed as he looked across briefly.

'You certainly have a vivid imagination. Somehow, I don't think Charles will buy any of those.'

'I'm sure you can think up something he'll believe.' She looked out at the passing scenery. 'It's only a short drive from London, but it's another world, isn't it?'

'Mmm!' Without taking his eyes off the traffic ahead of them, he said. 'I'm thinking of looking for somewhere around here myself. Not a house like Charles'; just somewhere to get away from it all at the weekends, with a couple of rooms for visitors.'

After passing through the next town, the volume of traffic lessened and Joanne guessed it wasn't far to the motorway. They'd soon be in London again, and that would be the end of it. She recalled his kissing her on the hill. She was still as confused about that as she had been at the time.

She came down to earth as the sound of scraping and screeching filled the air. For a fraction of a second, she saw the bodywork of a tractor that had exited from a gate on the left. Reacting as best as he could, Benedict had steered to the right. They scraped along the side of the tractor and slid past. Benedict lost control, and the car's underside dragged along the surface of the banking. Joanne was held firmly in place by the safety belt, but she still jerked about as the car sped on. Perhaps Benedict could have avoided the inevitable, and they would have come to a redeeming stop, if it hadn't been for a large drainage pipe, intended to ensure the continued flow of water in the ditch. It was their down-fall.

She wanted to scream, but nothing emerged. You were supposed to see your whole life pass in front of you in fractions of a second, but that didn't happen to Joanne. She heard Benedict yell, 'Hold on, hold on!' She grabbed the structure in front of her. It didn't help much. She felt the final thud and the crash. Bits and pieces flew around the interior and then, as the car shuddered and protested, the air bags exploded and a chilling silence descended. Joanne noted they were still the right side up, and she wondered if that was the end and she was about to die, before she lost consciousness.

She came to a few minutes later, and felt someone struggling to pull her out of the passenger seat. Still bemused and groggy, she did her best to co-operate, and eventually she tumbled out of the car onto the banking. Some blood was on the side of her face, but it wasn't a steady flow. The tractor driver, who had helped her out of the car, led her back towards the road, and she collapsed when they reached it. Her face felt burned, and her trousers were ripped, but she was alive. She stroked her cheek and her hand smeared with blood; she cleaned it off on her trousers. Her thoughts returned to Benedict. Where was he? The tractor driver had gone back into the ditch, to try to reach him. She cradled her head in her hands and waited.

When he came back, he was white in his face but his voice was steady. 'How do you feel?'

Joanne answered. 'Okay, I think. Nothing serious. What about Benedict?'

'Your friend? I don't know. He's unconscious, and he's bleeding. I can't get at him properly, the framework is twisted and I can't open the door. I don't want to drag him out via the other side. I might do more harm than good.'

Joanne nodded. A feeling of panic was stuck somewhere in her throat. She managed to gather enough strength to ask, 'He's not dead, is he?'

'No, he's definitely breathing, but unconscious. I'm going to call the emergency services. The sooner they get him out, the better. They know how to do it best. I don't want to risk trying anything myself.'

The relief she felt when she knew he

was still alive was tangible. She tried to catch her breath and steady herself. She nodded. He took his phone out of the bib of his dungarees and was soon explaining to some people on the other end what had happened. She tried to stand up but her legs were wobbly, and the tractor driver pushed her gently back into a sitting position.

Despite Benedict's hard shell and sharp attitude, and in spite of her struggle not to like him, Joanne suddenly realized that she did like him. Very much. He'd opened himself up to her a little when he met her up on the hill, and somehow she knew that was a special accolade. She now prayed that he'd be all right; anything else didn't bear thinking about.

The tractor driver went to his vehicle. It was jutting into the road at an angle. He returned with a smelly blanket. He wrapped it round her shoulders. Joanne was grateful. She was shaking and cold.

'I use it to cover the engine in winter, but it's the best I can do at present. Help will be here soon.'

Joanne tried a wobbly smile. 'Thanks.'

He started to explain to her, and to himself, what had happened.

'I checked the road before I started to pull out of the field and it looked all clear to me. Your car is silver and there was no hedging. The colour of the car and sunlight blinded me for a fraction of a second. I just didn't see you. Your car was there before I had time to react.' He ran his hand down his face. 'I hope to God he'll be alright.'

She was too busy hoping the same thing to comfort him. He wasn't a reckless driver, overtaking at the wrong moment, or approaching from the opposite direction too fast. She just patted his arm stupidly and then they heard the sound of sirens in the distance and both of them silently thanked heaven. The sight of the ambulance and the sound of police sirens reassured Joanne for a moment.

She struggled to sound sensible after they arrived. A young constable asked her how she was, and what had happened. She longed to follow the happenings in the ditch, but the policeman kept her busy with asking questions and noting her replies. She had to tell him all she could remember. One of the ambulance men joined them and he did an on-the-spot check for signs of concussion or any other serious injuries.

'You've cuts and scratches, but nothing too serious. You'll probably be bruised all over tomorrow, but you've been very lucky. A doctor at the hospital will check you over again, just in case.'

Joanne looked up the road briefly and noticed a policeman was cordoning off the road and directing any oncoming traffic down a side road. When she checked, they'd managed to get Benedict out of the car and he was on a stretcher.

'I'm okay. I'm more worried about Benedict.'

She went across to where they'd carried him up the banking. He was still unconscious and the side of his head and hair was matted in blood. She touched his face with the back of her hand; it was cold and there was no reaction.

One of the men said, 'He's definitely broken an arm. His pulse and heart rate are okay, so that's a good sign, but we need to get him to the nearest hospital straight away, as he could have more serious internal injuries. Jim will take you there too, in the other ambulance, and then you'll both be in the same place. You'll be able to find out more about how he's getting on once he's been properly examined.'

'He . . . he's not going to die, is he?'

She watched as they loaded Benedict into the ambulance and closed the doors. The man patted her arm.

'I don't think there is any life-threatening injury, no. Both of you have been damned lucky. The fact that he is still unconscious is the most worrying fact at the moment. From the state of the car on the driver's side, he could easily have ended up with much more serious injuries. He had a guardian angel, there's no mistake about that. Before we get going, is there anything you need from the car?'

She pulled herself together. 'My handbag was in the front. I'd like that, if you can find it, and our bags are in the back. They might be useful.'

He nodded and, with the help of a policeman, they wrenched open the boot of the battered car. Joanne pointed to her bag and to Benedict's. His briefcase was lying there too, and the borrowed Barbour jacket. There might be important papers in the briefcase and she had to return the jacket, so she took both of these too. The ambulance man picked up her belongings and she followed him.

A short time, and fast journey later, Joanne went through the process of another check at the hospital. They confirmed there was no sign of concussion and that her injuries were relatively minor ones. They wanted her to stay overnight, though, just to be sure.

Joanne waited in the corridor with their bags. As soon as she had the chance, she asked about Benedict, and was extraordinarily relieved to hear they had almost finished treating him and then he'd be sent on his way to a ward. He was still unconscious — although they expected him to regain consciousness soon — and he'd broken an arm and two ribs. He'd also dislocated his knee and had various cuts and bruises. There were no serious internal injuries. She handed the nurse Benedict's holdall.

After Joanne watched Benedict's bed rolling down the corridor, she sat with her bag and his briefcase, waiting to be taken to her own ward. Thinking sensibly again, she decided someone close to Benedict should know about what had happened. No one had asked her for details so that they could contact someone. They presumed he was her boyfriend, knew she wasn't badly hurt, and presumed she'd set the wheels in motion. The only person she knew to contact was Charles. Benedict wouldn't like it, but his parents should know what had happened, and someone needed to inform his company headquarters. He was intending to fly to Paris this evening. For a moment, she wondered where to get Charles' number, but then she remembered Benedict's briefcase. It wasn't locked, and to her relief it contained a leather-bound address book, as well as lots of business papers. She found Charles' number and he answered straight away. She explained what had happened and the shock was evident in his voice as he asked how they both were and how he could help.

'Will you get in touch with his parents, Charles? I can't find their names in his address book. Someone ought to inform his company too.'

'Yes, yes, I'll do that. I have their number somewhere; and I'll call Benedict's personal assistant this afternoon if I can get him. He'll need to sort out Benedict's appointments. I think Benedict was planning to go to Paris on business, wasn't he?'

Joanne didn't answer, but Charles didn't seem to notice.

'Are you sure you're alright? I can be there in less than an hour, if I can help.'

'That's good of you, Charles, but you

can't do much at the moment. They've just taken Benedict upstairs to recover. They've given me a sedative, so I expect I'll be asleep soon, too. They want to keep me in for observation until tomorrow morning. If you come now, both of us will be out for the count by the time you arrive. It would be more helpful if you could sort all the other things out.'

He paused for a second. 'Right! As long as there is no danger. Perhaps I'll drive down and tell his parents personally. They can phone and check on the situation later on, and I can drive them there tomorrow to visit him.'

'Yes, do that. I think if you can reassure them there is no life-threatening injury they'll be able to hang on at home until tomorrow. If they came now, they'd only be sitting around in the corridor all night. If they need reassurance about how Benedict is, they can phone and ask for the doctor on duty.'

'Yes, you're right. Which hospital? I'll get on to it straight away.'

She told him. Joanne was already

feeling the effects of the sedative, as she told him, 'I feel so much better now that someone else is involved. Thanks, Charles.'

'I'm so glad that you're both okay. It sounds like Benedict wasn't quite so lucky, but at least you're both in one piece.'

Someone was coming towards her with a wheelchair. She yawned audibly.

He laughed softly. 'Get some sleep, Joanne. I hope you'll feel a lot better tomorrow. It must have been a harrowing experience.'

8

Joanne didn't remember much after her conversation with Charles. It was only the second time in her life that she'd had a sleeping tablet. She was woozy for a couple of seconds when she woke next morning, but then things fell into place again. The ward sister checked how she was feeling and the doctor confirmed she was fit enough to leave. She had breakfast and got ready. She found out where Benedict's room was, and the nurse on duty said it was alright for her to visit him.

Carrying her holdall and his brief-case, she found the right door. Knocking softly, she stuck her head around the door and peeped inside. He was lying, immobile, with his eyes closed. He was in his own pyjamas, although they were awkwardly fastened because his left arm was in a bulky plaster. She left the bags next to the door and tiptoed across the room. His colouring was pale, but still quite healthy. Somewhere inside her, a weight lifted. She scrutinized the various scratches but couldn't find any stitches. She longed to reach out and touch him, but she thrust her hands into the pocket of the borrowed jacket instead.

She started to leave when he opened his eyes, saw her and said, 'Hi!'

She gave him a hesitant smile. 'Hi!'

His voice sounded normal. 'You're all right? I asked the nurse this morning where you were, but no one seemed to know anything, apart from the fact that you weren't badly hurt.'

'I'm fine. How are you?'

He moved awkwardly, but didn't attempt to sit up. She guessed his ribs hurt too much.

'It's not as bad as it all looks. Breathing is a bit painful, and my knee is swollen like a melon, but they keep telling me I've been very lucky.'

'You were. Your side of the car is completely wrecked.'

Giving her a lopsided grin, he tried to sound cheerful.

'Pity! I liked that car. It was less than half a year old.'

'I phoned Charles yesterday and asked him to contact your parents.'

The smile left his face. 'There was no need for that.'

She shrugged. 'I decided they were entitled to know. I didn't know if you needed to tell anyone else. I left it up to Charles.'

'Can't be helped now, I suppose.'

'Charles said he'd phone your assistant, so they already know what's happened at work.'

Feeling happier with that information, he nodded. 'I'll probably receive an appropriate bunch of flowers soon. I suppose it's better to get flowers in hospital than the funeral parlour.'

She stared at him for a moment. 'That is not funny, Benedict!'

He looked up. 'Perhaps not. I'm trying to look on the funny side of it all. Do you know that you have some fantastic bruises and scratches down the side of your face, in shades of purple and blue! They don't match your eyes, unfortunately.'

'I know. I saw myself in the mirror this morning. And I haven't any make-up to camouflage anything either. People will think I'm married to a wife-beater.'

'Who's being ironic now? Seriously, are you all right? It was a hell of a thing to happen. The first time I've ever been involved in a serious accident.'

'Me too. I'm fine, Benedict, honestly. The doctors have confirmed I can leave hospital, so I must be okay. I expect you're not as lucky?'

'No. They want to do some more tests this morning. One thing is for sure — as soon as I can move around under my own steam, I'll be out of this place like a shot.'

She was relieved to hear his usual, determined self, and she nodded.

'But I hope you'll be sensible enough to listen to the doctors if they want to keep you for a couple of days.' She turned towards the door, then remembered something. 'Oh! I brought your briefcase.

That's where I found Charles' telephone number — from your address book.'

He eyed her wordlessly for a moment, before saying in frosty tones, 'What the hell were you doing messing around in my briefcase? The stuff in there is highly confidential and sensitive.'

Joanne was quiet for a second, and swallowed hard. His tone was accusatory and aggressive.

'I needed Charles' telephone number. I hoped to find some kind of address book in there, and I did.'

He moved slightly and his brows furrowed. 'You should have kept your nose out of it! That's my private address book. You could have got the telephone number somewhere else, if you were so intent on interfering.'

Her voice rose and her anger grew. 'Interfering? What's that supposed to mean? I was only trying to help. I don't even know Charles' proper address to look for it from the usual sources. I wanted to act fast. I didn't realize if I touched your damned case that I was handling state secrets. I didn't look at a single one of the blasted papers. Why should I? Or do you think I pump up my income by being an industrial spy for the highest bidder?'

Pompously he commented, 'The contents of my briefcase are none of your concern.'

Feeling her temper rising, she retorted, 'You're absolutely right, I couldn't care less about the contents of your briefcase. If you want an apology, you have it. I clearly made a giant faux pas by trying to help. Perhaps I should have just left things alone, but I don't function like that. Unlike you, I think it is important to be helpful and kind. Do you know something, Mr North? You're the most ungrateful and irritating man I have ever met. You could have died in that crash yesterday — we both could have — yet all you can think about just hours later is how important the stuff in your briefcase is. I've never been gladder that we don't have to meet again.'

She fetched the briefcase from where

she'd left it, dumped it next to his bed, and turned on her heel.

He stared after her silently. The colour in his face drained away as he tried to lean forward. He lifted his hand but she was through the door before he had time to react verbally. He fell back into the pillow and muttered in frustration as he grew aware just how much his body was hurting.

* * *

She felt as if something had been crushed inside her, and fought the threatening tears. She was glad to be able to go into an empty visitors' room at the end of the corridor for a moment to regain her composure. She stared out of the window at the bustle of people down below until she felt calm again. She had to get back to work soon. Bill needed her help. She had to forget Benedict and get on with her life.

As she was crossing the main reception area, she spotted Charles coming towards her with someone at his side. Joanne guessed she was Benedict's mother. She straightened and managed a stiff smile when they met.

Charles was the first to speak.

'Good heavens, I thought you said you were fine? What happened to your face?'

Joanne automatically touched her cheek. 'It looks worse than it is. Nothing serious! I was very lucky.' She smiled at Benedict's mother.

'Dorothy, this is Joanne. Joanne, this is Benedict's mother.'

The older woman held out her hand and smiled. Joanne took it.

'Hello, Mrs North. I'm pleased to meet you, although I wish it had been under better circumstances.'

Dorothy North was tall and slim. She was dressed in good clothes of simple lines and neutral colours. Her salt and pepper hair was drawn back severely and trapped at the back of her head with a black bow, in a kind of mini-ponytail. She wore little make-up. Joanne noticed the resemblance between her and Benedict. Their eyes were the same colour, but his mother's were decidedly more benevolent.

'Hello, Joanne. I hope I can call you Joanne? Charles told me all about you and Benedict on the way here. I'm glad to meet you, and hope you really are alright after what happened?'

Joanne could only guess what Charles might have told her, so she just nodded. 'I'm fine.'

'How is he?' Dorothy's question, and her face, was full of anticipation and worry.

'I've just left him. He's still in bed, and I think they intend to do some more tests this morning, to be quite sure. I don't think they can do much about broken ribs. They'll have to heal on their own. He has one arm in plaster and apparently a badly swollen knee. He wasn't in a very good mood and was already talking about the quickest way to get out of hospital.' She tried to sound relaxed. 'You know what he's like. He doesn't like being ordered around. He prefers to be the one doing the ordering.'

Dorothy smiled. 'Yes, I know what he's like. He always was determined, and quite stubborn. It must be a kind of torture for him, to be kept in bed. The nurses have my sympathy.'

'Mine too!' Joanne looked at her watch. 'If you'll excuse me, I'm off to catch the next train back to London. I have to get to work.'

Charles cut in. 'Work? Must you? Surely you should take things easy for a day or two?'

'I phoned work just now to tell them I'd be very late, and I found that one of the others has 'flu, so they need my help badly. We have to get some important orders packed and ready by later on this afternoon. I feel quite fit, Charles. Don't worry! The hospital wouldn't have let me go if there was any doubt about that.'

Mrs North viewed Joanne with interest. 'What do you do, Joanne?'

'I help run a small warehousing company dealing in children's toys. There are only three of us, so it's bad enough if one of us is missing, let alone two.'

'Oh, I presumed you worked for Benedict!'

Joanne shook her head. 'No. I've never worked for Benedict, and I don't want to. I used to think I'd like to work in a dynamic company, until recently. I've only been in my current job a couple of weeks, but I've found that I love it. I can make decisions without involving anyone else, and I get on with the others really well.'

Dorothy North nodded. 'I won't keep you if you have to get back to work, but it is a pity we don't have time for a proper chat. We must meet again, as soon as Benedict is feeling better — and before he puts his nose to the grindstone once more.'

Joanne smiled, and met her friendly expression without agreeing or disagreeing to the suggestion. At the moment, she wouldn't care if she never saw Benedict North again, but she couldn't tell his mother that.

'He's in room three-eight-one. I have to rush. Bye!'

'Bye, my dear.'

'Bye, Joanne. See you soon I hope?' Charles tucked his hand under Dorothy's elbow, and they parted to go in opposite directions.

★ ★ ★

By the time she reached London and got to the warehouse, the day was well advanced. Bill was delighted to see her. He didn't give her time to catch her breath before he started telling her what had happened since he arrived that morning.

He stopped suddenly, and considered her more closely.

'Gosh, you took a hammering, didn't you? Are you sure you should be in work?'

Joanne smiled. 'It looks worse than it is. Just some aches and bruises. I'm alright, Bill. I imagine Sally feels a lot worse than I do. What can I do to help?'

'Tell me about the accident first. What happened?'

Joanne told him.

'It sounds like you had a lucky escape, even if your friend is still in hospital. You hear about some awful accidents, sometimes. I've been lucky. So far, touch wood, I've never been involved in one.'

'Neither had I. It was frightening at the time, but as soon as I knew neither of us had life-threatening injuries, I calmed down again.' She thrust her hands into the pockets of her trousers. 'Now, I'll pop upstairs and switch the office phone over to the answering machine, then come back down to do whatever you think I can manage.'

'If you're quite sure? I think I should cover Sally's job and do the orders that are due to be collected this afternoon. You aren't familiar with our storage systems or how to use the lift. It would be a waste of time for you to learn that now. If you can stay here in my little cubby to check any deliveries, that would be a great help. When a supply van arrives, just check that the items agree with the delivery note. Tell them to pile the stuff over there, against the wall. I'll sort it out and put it on the shelves when I have time. Don't go lifting heavy stuff, get the driver to do that.'

It sounded quite simple, so Joanne nodded.

'And can I do anything else while I'm waiting for someone to arrive?'

'See this pile of delivery notes?' He waved a sheaf of papers in the air. 'If you like, you can feed the details into the computer. If someone wants something that we do have, but doesn't appear on the system because it hasn't been entered, we'll get in a real mess and lose customers.'

Joanne nodded. 'That doesn't sound too difficult. At least I have an idea how to do that. Off you go. Carry on with sorting out the orders, and if I have a problem, I'll come and ask you.'

Bill nodded and hurried off towards the back of the building with a bundle of papers in his hand.

Later that afternoon, things calmed down. The day's deliveries were finished, and Bill had neat piles of goods near the door for the remaining customers to pick up. He handed her some handwritten lists of what had gone out, and to whom.

Joanne took them upstairs with her to the office, to feed into the computer. It was warmer up there, and after a well-deserved cup of coffee, she began to open the envelopes waiting for her attention on the desk, and check if there was anything urgent among the letters. There wasn't. She switched the answering machine to playback and leaned back in her chair with her hands encircling a comforting mug of rapidly cooling coffee. There was a call from one of their regular customers, ordering some toys. Joanne made a note of what he wanted. Next was a call from the bank, asking her to talk to them about a disputed payment from one of their customers. There was another call from an insurance company about renewing their fire policy. She stiffened when she heard Benedict's voice.

'Joanne, it's Benedict. Please call me back.'

It was surprising to hear him include the word 'please' in his message after the way they'd parted. His voice was curt and insistent. She hit the delete button. She had no intention of phoning him back. They had nothing to discuss.

By the end of the afternoon, and after deleting another call from Benedict, she was as glad as Bill to leave the building and head for home. She hadn't finished making herself a cup of tea before her telephone rang. She was in two minds whether to answer it, but then she saw that the incoming call was from Colleen.

'Hi!'

'Hi! And? What was it like? Did you enjoy the weekend?'

'It was a lot better than I expected it to be — until we had an accident on the way home.'

'An accident? What accident?'

Joanne proceeded to give her the details.

Colleen sounded worried. 'Are you okay? I can be with you in half an hour.'

'Yes, perfectly. But do come anyway! I'd love to see you. I'll make us something to eat.'

By the time Colleen arrived, she had macaroni cheese in the oven, and a mixed salad all ready and waiting.

Divesting her coat and throwing it over a vacant chair, Colleen took a deep breath.

'Mm! That smells yummy.' She took a look at Joanne. 'Wow! Your face is a right mess. Does it hurt very much? Any other injuries?'

They settled with their plates at the small kitchen counter, and Joanne told her about the weekend, and then about what had happened on the return journey, in more detail.

'Crikey! It sounds as if you were really lucky.'

'I was. Benedict, not so much.'

Someone knocking the door interrupted them. When Joanne opened it, she faced one of the biggest bunches of white roses she'd ever seen. Hidden behind them, until he tipped his head to the side to smile at her, was Charles.

'Hello, Joanne. Benedict told me to get you a bunch of flowers and bring them to this address.'

Joanne wouldn't be rude to Charles, but she didn't want anything from Benedict.

'Hello, Charles. Do come in. I'd like to throw the flowers in the bin, but that has nothing to do with you, and it's not fair to let flowers die, so I'll accept them.'

Charles studied her for a moment. 'I gathered that you two had a tiff, but I didn't ask what it was about.'

'Don't stand on the doorstep. Please — come in. Come and meet my friend, Colleen. She's the one I told you about, who's so interested in historical houses and such.'

Joanne took the flowers from Charles and went ahead of him into the small living room. Colleen looked up with interest and Joanne introduced them. She left them talking as she went to rummage in a cupboard for a container for the roses. In the end she decided she'd have to use a large, sealed flowerpot. The flowers looked good in the terracotta container, and she tweaked them into position.

As she carried them back to the living room, she heard Charles' laughter mixed with Colleen's. They seemed to be getting on like a house on fire. Joanne placed the delicate white blooms on a side table and joined them. Charles was sitting in a comfortable floral armchair opposite Colleen. He looked up.

'You have a nice place here, Joanne.'

'Nothing to compare to your house and its priceless contents, but we can't all live in stately homes, can we? I feel happy here, and I like the people who live upstairs. They have their own side entrance.'

'My home is a never-ending headache because of the running costs. Just heating the damned place in winter is enough to drive me to the brink of madness. It guzzles money. I have thought about giving up a couple of times, and trying to sell it, but it's been in the family for generations, and I have an awful feeling my ancestors will come back to haunt me for evermore if I do. So that means I'm caught between going bankrupt or living with ghosts for the rest of my life. To be honest, I do love the place, but I never reckoned with it being a never-ending drain to my bank balance. My father managed to keep it afloat, but I wonder if I'll be the last one of my family to live there. The death duties when I die will be horrific. At the moment, some distant second cousin will inherit it, and I'm sure he'll ditch it without giving it a second thought.'

Colleen asked, 'Is it open to the public?'

'No. Joanne mentioned you might like to see it, though, and I told her you can do so, anytime. I'd have to pay people to be on hand permanently if I opened it to the public. I already pay a daily house-keeper and a gardener, and a couple of people on a part-time basis to help with the cleaning and gardening, just to keep things going. The farms that belong to the estate are all leased out, so I don't need to worry about them, thank God!'

'Lots of former stately homes open their doors as venues for weddings, conferences, weekend courses and various other things. Some hold Christmas Markets in their grounds, or have regular historical, wine, or music festivals, and all kinds of other annual events. Have you ever thought of doing something like that to generate some extra income?'

He smiled at Colleen. 'No, I haven't, because I haven't got the time, or the know-how to do it. I run an art gallery to earn money, here in London.'

'Joanne told me how beautiful the house is. Launching things and making the right contacts is probably the hardest part. Then word of mouth takes over, and if you provide what people want, they'll keep coming back. Georgian houses are wonderful backgrounds for all kinds of events. If you're in London most of the time, though, that is a problem. You need someone on the spot.'

Colleen's eyes were sparkling, and Charles viewed her with growing interest.

Joanne brought them back to the present. 'We've just had something to eat, but there's plenty left over. Are you hungry?'

He lifted his hand. 'No, thank you. I'm not hungry. I took Benedict's mother out to a late lunch, before I drove her home again.'

Joanne nodded. 'She seems like a nice person. She doesn't have thousands of sharp edges sticking out of her everywhere, like her son does.'

Charles nodded. 'Somehow, I thought Benedict had done something wrong when he asked me to organize the flowers. Don't take too much notice of him when he's in that sort of mood. He forgets himself sometimes, because he's so used to ordering people around. Even I have to remind him occasionally that I am not one of his office drudges. He doesn't realize how bossy he sounds.'

'Huh! Don't make excuses for him. Politeness costs nothing. It wouldn't make him less successful if he managed to be courteous instead of acting like a bear with a sore head all the time.'

Charles laughed. 'You may not believe it, but Benedict is generally very well-mannered and civil, most of the time. Or at least, his business associates tell me so, and I believe them. You saw how well behaved he was this weekend. I didn't hear a single growl from him.'

Joanne shrugged. 'I've seen how uncivil he can be, though. I don't like it, and he knows that.'

'I know it sounds like I'm defending him, but he was in a lot of pain this morning when we saw him, and he isn't used to being dependent on other people for a single thing. He's very strong-minded and self-sufficient. Imagine how he feels, having to ask someone for help when he wants to go to the toilet. I don't know what he said to you, but give him the benefit of the doubt and excuse him. As soon as they gave him some painkillers, and he could sit up properly and breathe more easily, he calmed down a lot. There was a world of difference in him between when his mother and I arrived and when we left.'

Joanne suddenly realized that the present situation would give Benedict the ideal pretext to tell Charles that they'd finished. Charles knew they'd quarrelled, and also that she was angry with Benedict. It was perfect! She sidestepped Charles' plea and instead asked, 'Would you like something to drink?'

'Thanks, but another time perhaps. I haven't been home yet, and I hope my assistant in the gallery hasn't botched anything or driven a potential customer away in my absence.'

'If so, send the bill to Benedict. It's his fault. You've been his mother's chauffeur and his delivery service as well.'

'That's what friends are for. Under the circumstances, I'm sure he'd do the same for me.' He got up to go.

Colleen looked at her watch. 'I'll be off too. It would be good for you to get to bed early if you spent last night in hospital and worked today.'

'I'm okay, but it's not a bad idea. We've been busy in the warehouse all day; Sally was off ill.'

Colleen gathered her belongings and got up. 'There you are, then. I'll phone tomorrow to check on you.'

Joanne followed them down the narrow hall and they said their goodbyes. When she was back in the living room, she glanced out of the window and noticed Colleen and Charles were still talking in front of Charles' car. She turned away and smiled to herself.

★ ★ ★

True to her word, Colleen did ring the next evening.

'How are you today?'

'After a good night's sleep, I feel really fit. We were very busy in work again today, but it was okay. Sally hopes to be back sometime next week, so we are trying to keep things running smoothly until then.'

'Charles is nice, isn't he?'

'Yes, very. I liked him from the moment we met.'

Colleen dragged out the question she wanted to ask most of all.

'How much do you like him? You always insist that Benedict doesn't mean anything to you, so are you interested in Charles?'

Joanne laughed. 'No, I'm not. I like Charles, but I don't have any romantic feelings for him, if that's what you mean.'

There was a touch of relief in Colleen's voice. 'That's okay then, because he invited me to visit his gallery yesterday, before we parted company, and I wanted to be sure I wasn't treading on your toes. Oh, and I gather that Charles doesn't know anything about you being employed by the agency? My lips are sealed about that, don't worry.'

'Thanks, and it's no problem. Are you going? To the gallery?'

There was a moment's hesitation, but then Colleen said, 'Yes, I think I will. It's not far from our offices. I thought that if I popped over in my lunch hour, it wouldn't appear too pushy. If I went after work, he might feel he had to invite me for a drink or something.'

'You two seemed to hit it off from the word go, didn't you?'

'Yes, it was funny. I had the feeling I'd known him for ages. He's such an easy person to be with.'

'Agreed, and he's also well-mannered and kind. People with aristocratic backgrounds are often snobbish and snooty, but he isn't. Benedict told me that Charles' mother died when he was young, so perhaps that's softened his attitude to life and made him less patronizing.'

'That could be true, but I think the majority of people are always like they were. Their character is sometimes affected by what happens as they progress, but their basic personality never changes. A nice person remains nice, a cheat is always a cheat.'

Joanne laughed. 'You may be right.'

'What about Benedict. Will you be seeing him again?'

'I hope not. He's arrogant and unfeeling. I can't understand why Charles puts up with him.'

'Isn't there a line in Shakespeare somewhere, something like 'the lady doth protest too much'? You are usually very open-minded about people, but you've had a bee in your bonnet about Benedict ever since you met him.'

Automatically, Joanne supplied the information. 'That quote is from Hamlet, and I doth not protest too much. You'd think the same about him if you saw how he acts.'

'Someone as successful and rich as him is understandably wary. You don't need A-levels to figure out that the majority of people want something for nothing from him, or hope to use him to their own advantage. He's built a protective barrier around himself, and learned that to survive he has to be plainspoken. That's why he comes across as hostile and antagonistic. It's frustrating for you, but you have to give him a chance. You haven't known him long, and I'm sure he was impressed with you, otherwise he would never have sought your company again.'

'Why are you making excuses for him? You've never even met him.'

'Because I'm picking up your smoke signals and they tell me you are more interested in him than you care to admit. Your anger is too personalized. You could have refused to go with him last weekend, but you didn't. I think if you really disliked him that much, you would have refused outright. Your annoyance with him, and what he stands for, is purely superficial. Deep down, I think you are attracted. Why not? He's an interesting, outstanding personality.'

'Colleen, I don't like him! I was just a stopgap in his daily agenda. Someone he wanted for a partner, for appearances' sake.'

'You do like him, even though you won't admit it.'

Joanne laughed. 'You have a very vivid imagination, and an innocent belief in happy-ever-after. I am not looking for any man, and even if I was, Benedict North would be the last one I'd consider.'

'I'm not so sure about that. Oh — I must go, I have a pie in the oven and if I don't rescue it soon, I'm going to end up with charcoal remains. Bye!'

9

Next morning, Joanne could afford to leave Bill to cope on his own. There were no deliveries expected until late afternoon, so he could handle the orders and she could get on with her office work.

She was interrupted after an hour. Bill called and she opened the office door.

'Joanne, there's someone here to see you.'

'Me?' Not many people knew where she worked, so she was stumped. 'Who is it?'

'I didn't ask. I just told him to wait in my office and I'd fetch you. I need to check something out the back.'

'Okay. I'm coming.' She clattered down the steps and crossed the space to Bill's little cubbyhole of an office. Opening the door, the breath caught in her chest when she saw Benedict sitting in the swivel chair in front of the desk.

'What are you doing here?'

He managed to look uncomfortable for a moment, and there was silence as they viewed each other.

'If the mountain won't come to Mohammed, Mohammed must go to the mountain.'

Her lips tightened.

'The very first thing I want to say is, I'm sorry for the way I acted that morning in the hospital. Charles told me that you liked the flowers, but remain angry with their sender.'

The colour rose in her face. She straightened, and crossed her arms in front of her.

'You probably don't even know what kind of flowers he bought.'

He grinned wickedly. 'You're wrong there. I told him to get white roses. I am always careful about sending any woman flowers. I've learned that the wrong gesture can be misinterpreted. White roses are symbolic of a fresh start, among other things.'

'You needn't have bothered!'

His expression steadied. 'I'm afraid you caught me at a bad moment when you told me about my briefcase and the address book. I do know I can trust you. My excuse is that I felt very uncomfortable and sorry for myself at that moment.'

'A bad moment? Do you have any good moments, Benedict? If you do, you clearly don't want me to witness them.'

He ran his hand down his face. 'You don't intend to make it easy for me do you? I'm trying to say I'm sorry! If you knew me better, you would also know that I don't try to be deliberately rude, unless someone deserves it. I know my temperament gets me into hot water sometimes. I'll try to reform!'

Remembering what Charles had said about how much pain he had been in, she grudgingly said, 'Okay, apology accepted. But you didn't have to come all this way to tell me that.'

'You ignore my telephone calls. I had no other choice but to come personally.

And I do have another reason.' He managed to look sheepish. 'I'm hoping you'll come to my flat on Sunday, for lunch.'

Her eyes widened in shock and she opened her mouth, but he forestalled her.

'I know I'm asking a lot of you, again, but my mother met you at the hospital and she clearly approves. She went home and told my father I'd seen the light. She even persuaded him it was time to bury the hatchet and come up to London with her to see me. They intend to come straight after he's held morning service.'

Exasperated she asked, 'Why didn't you tell her the truth — that we're not together?'

'Because Charles was there and I couldn't think of anything plausible at the time. She seemed so happy at the prospect of meeting you again. I didn't want to disappoint her. I don't get on with my father, but my mother is a gem. She's met other girlfriends of mine from time to time, but she never took to any of them in the way she seems to have instantly taken to you.'

'We hardly spoke a couple of sentences. I only met her on my way out.'

He shrugged. 'I think she can identify with you. She probably saw that you're less complicated than other girlfriends of mine she's met. More down-to-earth, less sophisticated.'

'Gee, thanks! You make me sound like I just fell out of a haystack with straw sticking out of my hair.'

'I didn't mean that, and you know it. You're good-looking and act normal in comparison to what she's got used to. You've caught her imagination, and I think she's beginning to hope for the patter of tiny feet sometime in the future.' He smiled and the cleft in his chin became more prominent.

She ignored the smile, but felt her resistance was crumbling; she was annoyed that he had this effect on her. Every time she saw him, something inside wanted her to throw caution to the wind, even though he drove her mad. She also knew that getting involved with Benedict North could only end in heartache. Colleen's remarks had been spot on. Her feelings for him weren't negative; her resentment and fractiousness were her defence. She was sure he'd take advantage of her as soon as he noticed she was giving way. She didn't want to end up with a broken heart.

She tried to ignore the butterflies in her stomach. She was close enough to notice the small lines at the corner of his grey eyes, and the subtle effect of his aftershave again. It brought back the memory of their kiss.

She suddenly recalled that she hadn't asked how he was. The scratches and bruising were healing. His cheekbones seemed more defined and he looked paler than she remembered.

'I'm sorry, I should have asked how you're doing.'

He shrugged. 'I'm okay. Ignoring all good medical advice.'

Joanne noticed the crutch leaning against the desk, and that his arm was hidden inside a dark blue support. 'How did you get here? You can't drive can you?'

'No. The knee is still playing me up, but it's improving. A masseur comes every day to speed things along. It hurts like hell, but it is doing me good. The arm is less of a problem than it might have been, because I'm right-handed, although it's still very annoying. I misappropriated a company car and chauffeur to bring me here.' His forehead displayed a tight frown. 'So, what do you say to Sunday lunch?'

Trying to ignore the attraction, and smothering the compassion she felt, Joanne said, 'This has got to stop, Benedict. You have to stop presuming I'm available whenever it suits you, and you have to stop lying to everyone about our relationship. Have you thought about the fact that we have a perfect alibi? Charles knows we had a quarrel that day. You only have to tell him it led to a final break up.'

Annoyance gleamed in his eyes. 'That

doesn't solve the problem of placating my mother. If you knew her, you would know she hangs on like a bulldog until something is settled.'

'Does she? It shows where your determination comes from, doesn't it? And I still don't see why you can't tell your mother the same thing — that we had a quarrel that day.'

'It's not that simple. I thought after the weekend at Charles' place I would be able to tie things up. I'd intended to tell him it was a passing episode and that we found out we didn't match.' He paused for a moment and eyed her calmly. 'Actually, between you and me, I was surprised to find that we get on better than I expected; and that's despite the fact that we shared the same bedroom and nothing happened, which is even more surprising.' He noticed her expression and returned to the point under discussion. 'But then the accident happened, and now my mother's met you, and she won't stand for a little thing like a quarrel being the end of it. She'll just go on at me to make it up to you.'

Biting her lip, she considered what he was saying. She was trapped by her own longings.

'I gathered from Charles that you don't get on with your father, so it shouldn't be that difficult to put them off. If you're at loggerheads with your dad, a meeting with your current girlfriend won't mean anything to him, will it?'

The skin on his cheek tightened. 'I'm not talking about my father. My mother is the problem. She's convinced that the appearance of a decent girlfriend will steady my everyday life, and might even help to patch things up between my father and me. She's got the bit between her teeth about you being my girlfriend, and she's not about to let it go so easily. I'd put up with a lot to please her.'

'They are your parents, whether you like it or not. Your father probably manoeuvred himself into a corner and didn't want to lose face by admitting he was wrong about you.'

He drew a deep breath and muttered,

'You don't know what you're talking about.'

'Perhaps, but half a lifetime of disregarding each other is wasteful and destructive. You should bury past differences. He's a vicar isn't he? I know that he had different ideas about what he thought was good for you, and how your future should be, but from the moment you proved yourself, he must have known he was wrong. He's very likely just as stubborn as you are. Someone has to take the first step. I bet it hurts your mother to see the two of you at loggerheads all the time.'

Seeing a chance of undermining her resistance, he said, 'Come on Sunday and see for yourself. I don't want to hurt her and I don't want to disappoint.' His mouth was unsmiling and his expression was concentrated and stiff.

Joanne tried to assess the situation sensibly. She found herself thinking that if she went, she might be able to do something to smooth the situation between the two men. On the other hand, it was absolutely none of her concern. He was someone who could be as flexible in his business dealings as was needed, but remained stiff-necked and proud with regards to his own father.

She saw the look of frustration while he waited for her answer. It made her wonder if he'd give up and walk out. She didn't want him to walk away. She didn't want their wobbly friendship to end, because she liked him too much. She was searching for a credible motive to surrender without him sensing she'd do anything for him. She had no reason to agree to his plans — apart from the knowledge she was helping him, and that was the best possible reason of all. She stood in front of him and looked down at the floor.

'Okay, I'll come. As long as you promise not to make a scene with your father.'

'I never do.'

To her surprise, he reached out for her hand and placed a kiss in her upward-turned palm. The gesture staggered her

219

and the feeling of molten fire that shot through her being alarmed her even more. She had never experienced such an instantaneous physical reaction to a mere touch before. She presumed it wasn't a characteristic gesture for someone like Benedict. It was too personal, too chivalrous. Any hint of contact they'd had up to now — the kiss on the hill, the occasional hug during the weekend — had been playacting for the benefit of others, but this . . . She tried to hide her confusion and hoped he didn't notice her bewilderment.

He struggled to get up, while keeping his weight on his healthy leg. She had to stop herself from helping — if she put her arms around him, it would give him the chance to study her face close up, and she was still too bewildered for that. By the time he had the crutch in position, Bill came in.

'Oh! Sorry, I thought you'd have finished by now.'

Benedict hastened to say, 'We have.' He started to make his way awkwardly across the room. Joanne bunched her fist and stood aside.

Bill was quick off the mark. 'Here, let me help you, governor. Where's your car?'

Joanne was expecting a bluff reply, but he surprised her by saying, 'Outside, on the opposite side of the road. If I could lean on you, that would be a great help. I haven't come to terms with the crutch yet. I don't think I ever will.'

Bill laughed. 'You've got yourself into a right mess, haven't you? I presume you're the chap who was with our Joanne in that crash? She came out of it in a better shape than you did.'

Benedict looked at her. 'Yes, I was with her. I'm glad she is still in such good shape.' There was teasing laughter in his eyes. 'I'll send you an email with the details, Joanne. I'm working from home at the moment, because I can't face hobbling back and forth to the office and getting people's sympathetic comments all the time.' He rummaged in his pocket and handed her his card.

'Just in case you've thrown my number in the bin!'

Joanne took it and nodded dumbly. When they were alongside each other, he faltered for a moment and leaned across to kiss her cheek.

'Thanks for everything,' he murmured.

Bill waited patiently. Benedict nodded to him, and tightened his grip on Bill's arm while manoeuvring with the crutch on the other side. Joanne watched them as they went out.

They left the office and Bill opened the main door to make things easier. Joanne watched as they went clumsily across the road to where a chauffeur was holding the car's rear door open. Benedict said something to Bill. Bill tipped the peak of his cap and came back. Joanne watched the BMW until Bill came into his office again.

'He's had a hammering, hasn't he? He seems like a decent chap, even though he has a bob or two to spare.'

Joanne pulled herself together. 'Yes,

that's true. I'd better get back to the office to clear up some of the backlog. Everything okay down here?'

'All okay at the moment.'

'Good! Why don't you come up for a cup of coffee, in about half an hour? I'll be finished with checking the monthly payments by then.'

'Will do. I've a couple of deliveries coming, but we're relatively quiet this morning.'

As she took the steps two at a time, she was still wondering if she'd been sensible to agree to Benedict's request. She ought to have refused to have anything further to do with him. But she wanted to see him again, even though it was pointless. The mere touch of his lips on her hand or on her cheek had only made her want more; a lot more.

10

He emailed her directions to his place, and she wasn't surprised to see the address was in the Docklands. Joanne figured lunch would be roughly one o'clock, so she planned to get there by about twelve-thirty. If his parents left for London straight after the morning service, they would reach the flat by twelve at the earliest. She wanted to give them some time on their own.

She dressed carefully in a taupe dress that was shaped but not too tight. It had three-quarter length sleeves and a draped bodice. She didn't have much jewellery, but her watch was a good one, and she added a simple gold chain she'd received for her eighteenth birthday. The traffic was quiet on Sunday morning and the underground was pleasantly empty. Leaving the nearest tube station, she looked up at the deep blue sky visible above the buildings. She walked briskly for a while towards her target. As she passed some greenery on the way, she heard the chatter of birdsong. Clearly the birds were also happy about the sunshine so late in the year. She took a deep breath as she approached the block in question. The external appearance had been left as original as possible, but some of it was a glittering mass of glass and steel. Without any real knowledge, she guessed a flat in one of the blocks would most easily cost a million and more. There was a concierge behind a shiny desk in the vestibule.

'Good morning, Miss. May I help you?'

'I'm expected. Joanne Courtland for Benedict North.'

He checked a list in front of him and nodded. 'The lifts are straight ahead. Third floor, down the corridor to the right.'

She straightened her shoulders and went ahead. The door opened silently on the third floor and she tried to banish the feeling of tension. It was bad enough to know she'd be facing Benedict again in a moment. On top of that, she was to meet his father, and pretend Benedict and she were in a relationship. A knot formed in her stomach as she pressed the brass bell.

In a matter of seconds the door flew open and she faced Benedict's mother.

'Come in, Joanne. It's lovely to see you again. I told Benedict to stay seated. By the time he'd hobbled to the door, you might have given up and gone away.'

A smile tipped the corner of Joanne's mouth. 'I bet he liked hearing that.'

Mrs North gestured to a niche with a clothes' rail. 'Hang your coat up. You know your way around. We're in the living room.'

Joanne hurried to comply — she didn't want to lose sight of Dorothy, as there were a couple of doors leading off the hallway, and if she was supposed to be Benedict's girlfriend, she ought to know where the doors led!

She caught up with his mother and they went into a room that had a wall of glass. The view was stunning. She tried not to look too impressed and went across to Benedict, who was sitting on a white leather couch, opposite another man on a twin couch. An oval glass table separated them. She bent down and gave Benedict a brief kiss on his cheek. Their eyes met and to her annoyance she found herself starting to blush.

'Morning, Benedict. How are things this morning?'

His eyes widened in approval and he responded with a cheerful, 'Better than yesterday, thanks. The daily massage is doing me a world of good, and the masseur thinks I'll be able to put my full weight back on it next week. Joanne, this is my father.'

Joanne turned her attention to the man opposite. She leaned across the table and offered her hand.

'How do you do? It's a pleasure to meet you.'

He was tall, almost as tall as Benedict. He also had compelling eyes like his son, only Benedict's were grey and his were a watery blue. He had a thin face, and grey hair. There was an inherent strength in his face and she could imagine that he might have a lot of the traits she'd also discovered in Benedict.

He got up and took her hand.

'Good morning. I'm pleased to meet you. My wife told me how you met as you were leaving the hospital.'

Joanne gave him an encouraging smile. 'Yes, very briefly. I was on my way back to work.'

His mother handed her a glass of sherry. 'Alright?'

Joanne nodded. 'Thank you.'

Mr North asked, 'What do you do? I hope you don't think I'm being too curious, but my job has turned me into someone who is always curious. I automatically ask questions, because I find it puts people at ease if they can talk about themselves.' He gave her the beginnings of a smile. She heard Benedict muttering something to himself softly in the background.

'I can imagine! I work for a company selling toys. It's a wholesale company. We purchase toys and then offer them elsewhere.'

'Do you like your job? Is it one of Benedict's companies?'

She noted that he knew Benedict had more than one. 'Yes! I like it very much.' She took a sip of the sherry and it slipped down her throat like molten honey. 'And no, it has nothing to do with Benedict, thank goodness!'

Mr North smiled, and his features softened noticeably.

Joanne said, 'You've come direct from morning service?'

'Yes. Someone else is filling in for me this evening. Are you a churchgoer?'

Joanne reasoned there were limits to how much you should lie. 'No, not any more. I stopped going regularly when I went to university. Our parish didn't offer much for youngsters when I was at home, but there was a youth club that was fairly successful. I went there for a while. I don't know if it still exists.'

He nodded. 'It's the same everywhere. It is difficult to make young people realize they need religion. I don't mean the 'down on your knees' kind, I mean the support and backing that the church can provide in your daily life. When things go wrong, for example!'

Joanne shrugged. 'It's a very commercial world these days, isn't it? I don't know the answer to how the church can attract people. I don't even know what would encourage me to go to church regularly again. There are undoubtedly people out there who would make an effort if ideas and ideals were more convincing. The church often seems more occupied with itself than with its followers.' She looked at him and smiled in earnest, and was surprised to see him smile back without a trace of animosity.

Joanne noticed that Benedict kept quiet most of the time, and he was obviously making an effort. The brunt of the conversation was borne by his mother and Joanne. They kept things running smoothly with news of people Benedict used to know, and information about Joanne's work and hobbies. Benedict had arranged for caterers to provide the meal, and by the time they announced that lunch was served, the atmosphere was still stress-free, and they all agreed that the food was delicious.

Joanne was surprised how quickly the time passed. They lingered over a cup of coffee. She checked her watch and decided she'd been with them long enough.

'I must go. I told you about my promise to meet Colleen this afternoon, didn't I Benedict?' He looked a little surprised but hid it well and nodded. She addressed his parents on the other side of the table. 'I promised to go to an exhibition with her before I knew you were coming today. I hope you'll excuse me?'

His mother smiled. 'Of course. We'll be leaving ourselves soon. It gets dark early at this time of the year, and I must be honest, I don't like being on the motorway when it's dark.'

Joanne got up and folded her serviette. She left it by the side of her plate. Leaning towards Benedict, she intended to kiss his cheek — but he moved his face slightly at the last moment, and their lips met. The effect of his lips on hers, even for a brief moment, left her burning with desire. She felt heady and confused as they gazed silently at each other for a second. The smile in his eyes contained a sensuous flame. She had to remind herself this was a man who was practiced in wrapping women round his fingers.

His father cleared his throat and brought her back to reality. She straightened quickly, and with heightened colour in her cheeks she reached her hand out across the table and said goodbye to him and Mrs North.

'Hope to see you again soon, Joanne.'

Confused and not knowing what to say, she just smiled and picked up her bag. Without any more words in Benedict's direction, she walked towards the door, and was relieved to escape. His voice, with a touch of laughter in it, drifted over his shoulder towards her. 'Bye, Joanne. I'll be in touch. Take care!'

She was glad to be outside the flat, and hurried down the corridor to wait for the lift. She leaned her forehead against the wall for a moment and wished she didn't feel so bewildered by his behaviour. It would have made things a lot easier for her if he'd kept everything as impersonal as possible. Under the circumstances, a peck on the cheek would have sufficed.

On the ground floor, the doors of the lift slid open silently, and she set off across the black marble vestibule. There was a very smartly dressed woman talking to the concierge. She had beautifully-cut, jet-black hair, perfect make-up and a grey costume that screamed money and quality. Joanne couldn't help but catch some of the conversation.

'I'm sorry, Madam but you are not on Mr North's list of regular guests. I'll have to phone and ask if I can let you through. Your name is . . . ?'

'Bonnaire, Adrienne Bonnaire. Benedict and I are old friends.' Her English was excellent, but she had a strong French accent.

'Nevertheless, I'll have to ask. It would cost me my job if I allowed anyone to walk in and visit a resident without their permission.'

Joanne wondered if this woman was one of Benedict's former paramours. She recalled Charles mentioning a former long-lasting girlfriend in France. If she was, and she turned up at his door now, his parents would find it odd — especially if they'd met her in the past. They'd just shared lunch and said goodbye to someone they thought was his present girlfriend. She hesitated for a split second, but decided she had nothing to lose.

'Good afternoon, Madame Bonnaire. I'm a friend of Benedict and I just left. His parents are still visiting him. It's none of my business, and I'm not saying you shouldn't visit him, but I thought you might like to know.'

The concierge had the telephone receiver in his hand. With raised brows, Adrienne considered Joanne for a moment, and then made an impatient cutting gesture in his direction before she told him, 'No, don't bother! If his parents are with him, it will be more sensible to contact him later on.' She turned to Joanne. 'You are . . . ?'

'My name is Joanne Courtland.'

'And you've just been visiting Benedict at the same time as his parents?'

'Yes.'

Adrienne's brows lifted and she caught hold of Joanne's arm. 'My word, this is interesting! I'd like to hear more. Will you come with me for a cup of coffee? My curiosity is aroused. Do say yes!'

Joanne was nonplussed, but there was something endearing about the woman. Her eyes twinkled and she tilted her head in expectation of Joanne's answer. The cloud of jet-black hair swished and fell perfectly into place again. A moment later it was slightly out of place because of her tilted head. Joanne realized she was just as curious to find out who Adrienne was. She had no other plans for the day, so she nodded.

'Yes, why not.'

'Good. There's a decent-looking place not far from here, in the basement of one of these blocks.'

Feeling adventurous alongside this exotic creature, Joanne nodded to the concierge, and kept pace with Adrienne as they headed towards the entrance. Just as they were leaving, another person came in. Joanne was surprised to see it was Vanessa — and Vanessa was clearly just as surprised to see her.

She was the first to speak. 'Joanne! What are you doing here?'

Joanne thought briefly that as far as Vanessa was concerned, she was Benedict's latest girlfriend. Why should she be surprised? 'Visiting Benedict, of course.'

'That's what I was planning to do.'

'His parents are there. I've just left them all.'

Adrienne studied their exchange silently.

'That's okay. They won't mind me. I've met his mother several times.'

Flustered by her declaration of familiarity, Joanne said, 'The concierge will need to announce you.'

Looking smug, Vanessa replied, 'Benedict put me on his list of accepted guests ages ago. I don't need to be announced. Bye, Joanne. 'Til next time.' She swept past them, and Joanne watched as she approached the concierge, said something, and was waved on. With a triumphal backward glance in their direction, Vanessa headed for the lift.

Adrienne watched the happening speculatively, and brought her back to the present.

'Come, Chéri! I think we have a lot to talk about, don't we?'

The bistro was elegant and discreet. There were quiet, leather niches and the service was perfect. Adrienne arranged her belongings at her side and beckoned a waiter.

'What would you like?'

Joanne shrugged. 'A cappuccino.'

Adrienne nodded. 'Two cappuccinos.' The man left them and Adrienne leaned forward. 'Now, tell me who you are. You know Benedict, so we have that in common. Are you his present sweetheart?'

Joanne hesitated, but then managed, 'In a way.'

'And what does that mean?'

Joanne studied the other woman's face and liked her instinctively. 'You know Benedict well?'

She chuckled.

'Oh yes, we were very close five or six years ago.'

Joanne looked down.

'I suppose the English would say we had an affair. Perhaps I should explain more fully, then you might trust me a little more. I used to be an actress. I played theatre in Paris and had supporting roles in a couple of films. I met Benedict at a party. We got on from the minute I met him. I liked his typically English conservative art and admired his ambition. I'm a lot more extroverted, so we complemented each other. I also loved his humour and his generous nature. We met on and off for a couple of months. It wasn't easy to meet because I was often on tour, or making a film outside Paris somewhere. Benedict was still establishing himself in the business world. After a couple of months, we both came to the conclusion it was pointless to continue it. There was little romance involved.'

The waiter returned with their coffee and she paused for a moment, before continuing, 'Neither of us felt the kind of spark that told us it was the kind of love that would last. I was a stopgap, and so was he.' She took a sip of the coffee. 'Strangely enough, we parted the best of friends. We have met from time to time since then, but merely as friends. Benedict even visits my husband and me. I met my husband at another party and knew straight away he would be the love of my life. He inherited a title, a rundown chateau and a vineyard. He now produces some of the best wines in Europe and has restored his family home to its former glory. Benedict was a real friend and lent Jacque some money to tide us over, until things started to improve. You can't produce good wines overnight.'

'And did your husband know about your past relationship with Benedict?'

'Naturally! We all have a past, Chéri, and Jacque knows how much I love him. I tell him so, constantly. Surprisingly, despite being very different, the two of them get on well. Jacque loves parties, entertaining, meeting new people, travel, organising events. Benedict always hated those kinds of things.'

Joanne nodded. 'So you are happy?'

'Yes, blissfully. I love the role I have at Jacque's side. We have a little girl, Collette, and she is our treasure! She's two. I left her with her nanny this afternoon and thought I'd take the opportunity to say hello to Benedict again. We are in London for Jacque to attend some meetings, but he went to Bristol this morning to organize sales with someone there. I decided to wait for him here with Collette. He'll be back tomorrow morning, and then we return home the day after that.'

'I see!'

'And you? What is your connection to Benedict? The other woman who came in to Benedict's apartment building when we left — she didn't seem too pleased to see you, and you didn't seem happy to see her either.'

'Was it so obvious? Oh, dear. In all honesty, I don't have any claim on Benedict, in any way.' Joanne felt she could trust Adrienne. She explained how they had met, and how things had got more complicated in time.

Adrienne laughed. 'Good heavens! I would never have thought that Benedict had need of a dating agency. The women always buzzed around him like bees around the honey. It's nothing to do with his money, and he isn't outstandingly handsome. My Jacque is handsomer. But Benedict has the kind of charisma that will remain with him all his life. I can't find the words to describe it, it is just part of him.'

Joanne nodded.

'How long have you been working for this agency?' Adrienne asked.

'I only went on the one assignment for them, with Benedict. I finished almost straight after because I found myself another job.'

'And that was the only engagement via this agency, the one with Benedict?'

'Yes.'

She clapped her hands. 'And you've been seeing him since then? Oh, how romantic! I can understand why Benedict fell for you.'

'He didn't fall for me. Things got complicated and we got caught up in a net of deception.' Joanne explained about Charles, and the accident, and meeting his parents.

Adrienne looked at her dubiously. 'I'm not so convinced that you're indifferent to him. Not many women are, once they've met him.' Joanne coloured, and she played with her cup. 'From your expression, and the atmosphere back at his apartment building, I think you may

love him more than you want to admit.'
She shrugged. 'It is perfectly understand-
able; Benedict is special. There is more to
this than mere complication, and meetings
of convenience. It's almost unbelievable.'

Joanne had not been confronted so
directly with admitting or denying her
true feelings, but in some small way it
was a relief to finally acknowledge them
out loud to this woman.

'I like him, of course I do, but I have
no intention of getting involved with him.
I don't want to fall in love with him and
end up dejected, disappointed and re-
jected. I didn't like all the dishonesty,
but Benedict kept persuading me that
circumstances meant we had to keep up
the pretence. I was always too weak to
refuse. He doesn't think of me in any
other way than as the woman he paid to
accompany him one evening.'

Her eyebrows lifted. 'That's your sup-
position. Benedict is not someone who
acts irresponsibly. Never! The accident
was not planned, of course not, but he
seems to have even used that to his own

advantage and involved you in this business of meeting his parents today. I didn't know about the accident. Mon Dieu! That must have been frightening.'

'I was luckier than Benedict. That's why he is at home a lot at the moment, and I think that is why his mother thought it might be a chance to smooth the stormy waters between him and his father.'

Adrienne looked puzzled. 'His father?'

'They don't get on very well. His father wanted Benedict to do something completely different with his life. You didn't know that?'

'Only vaguely. Benedict never talked about his family, and he never met mine either. My father would have skinned him alive! He thought I was an innocent until I met and married Jacque.' She shifted in her seat. 'This is very interesting! You know more about Benedict than I ever did, and he isn't bothered that you've got so involved in his personal life. He wouldn't have asked you to meet his parents if he was wary about

244

the consequences. That means he's more interested in you than you imagine. Know something? I'm so intrigued, I'm going back to find out more about all of this.'

Joanne lifted her hand in panic. 'No, please! Don't ask him about me. That would be so embarrassing. I've only helped him out a couple of times. I don't mean anything special to him. His mother wanted to meet me again. Benedict was only humouring her when he asked me to come to lunch. I'm hoping that everything will go back to normal now. Benedict will be able to return to his work soon, and he can tell everyone we've had a fight, and then there'll be no reason for us to meet again, there'll be no reason to go on pretending to his parents, or anyone else, and everyone can carry on with their lives as if I'd never got involved.'

'Who was that woman who waltzed past us on her way to his flat? What role does she play in his life?'

'Her name's Vanessa. They've known each other for years, but I don't know how involved the friendship is. I think she'd like to be someone special in his life, but Benedict has never talked about her to me, so I don't know how serious the friendship is.'

Adrienne's eyes lit up. 'Oh, I'm so glad I came this afternoon! Benedict and I don't see each other very often any more, but when Jacque arranged all these meetings in London, I thought it would be a good opportunity to catch up. I thought I'd surprise him.'

Joanne laughed softly. 'I imagine it will be a surprise. It sounds like you get on with him very well.'

'I do, I do. It was a pity we didn't make it, because Benedict is quite special, but my Jacque is absolutely heavenly, and we have our Collette, so I really don't regret a thing. I won't compromise you or give anything away, I promise, but I'm interested in hearing Benedict's version of all this.'

'Please, don't fish for information. I just filled a purpose in his life for a while.'

She looked closely. 'But you like him, don't you? You English are so complicated. I don't see what's wrong in telling someone you like them. It would do someone like Benedict the world of good. You don't have to use the word love. Love is something that grows slowly and sweetly, and it is often rooted in the growing knowledge about each other, appreciation of what you are like and your shared experiences. But it has to start somewhere.'

Joanne coloured. 'I'm not even sure I could tell him I like him. I think a lot of people tend to butter him up because of what he represents and owns. I don't want him to think I'm like that. I'm not. We tend to shout at each other a lot.'

Adrienne clapped her hands together again. 'Wonderful! I could never get Benedict upset about anything.' She got up and picked up her things again. 'I won't give you away, but I am intrigued and would like to know more. Give me your telephone number. If I can get some information out of him, I'll keep you in the picture.' She ruffled through her bag and finally found a pen. While Joanne was writing, she asked, 'What do you do? Do you work in one of Benedict's companies?'

She shook her head vigorously. 'Everyone keeps asking me that! No. I run a small warehouse dealing in toys. I like what I'm doing. I'm determined to make a success of it, for the owner and people who work there.'

Adrienne viewed her speculatively. 'I hope we meet again, Joanne. You're beautiful, clever, and unassuming. I understand why Benedict might be attracted.' She grabbed her belongings, and Joanne's telephone number, written on a coaster. She came around and kissed Joanne, French fashion, then left, winding her way through the bistro tables, on four-inch heels, as if she was on the catwalk. She turned and lifted her hand at the exit. Joanne was left feeling slightly dazed.

She watched the petite figure heading back in the direction of Benedict's flat. She wondered what would happen if

Vanessa was still there when Adrienne arrived. Did Vanessa know about Adrienne's part in Benedict's past? After a minute or two, Joanne paid the bill for some of the most expensive coffee she'd ever had and hoped she wouldn't meet anyone else on her way home.

★　★　★

Later that evening, Joanne spoke to Colleen for the first time in several days. She brought her up to date on what had happened since they last spoke. Joanne suggested they should meet again soon to have a proper chinwag. There was a moment of hesitation from Colleen.

'Are you too busy at the moment? Is there a new boyfriend on the horizon? Come on, you can tell me! Something has happened I don't know about.'

'Well . . . actually, it's Charles.'

'Benedict's friend, Charles?' Joanne was surprised, but then again, when she thought about it, they were very well suited.

'Yes. We hit it off from the start. I went to see his gallery one lunch hour, and he asked me out for a drink that evening. We just sat and talked for hours. I can't even remember what we talked about.'

Joanne laughed softly. 'I like Charles, you know that. He is such a nice person. I can imagine you two getting on. I'm so pleased for you. Charles isn't the fly-by-night type you've gone for in the past. You have a lot in common.'

Colleen's voice bubbled. 'Yes, we do. I'm going down to his house next weekend.'

'You'll love it. It is all the things that you adore. History, beauty, fantastic architecture. It wouldn't still be in such good condition if his family hadn't been determined to take care of it, generation after generation. It's obvious that Charles loves it, despite all the headaches it gives him.'

'I'm so excited about seeing it — you know how potty I am about old houses — but I'm even more excited about seeing Charles. And I have you to thank for it! If you hadn't met Benedict, I wouldn't have met Charles. Are things still so complicated between you two?'

'Yes, but I'm hoping it will all sort itself out really soon now. I keep telling Benedict he should just tell everyone the truth. I'm hoping, now that I've played along with him and met his parents as he wished, he'll pull my neck out of the noose, and let me get on with my life again. There's no real reason why Benedict can't tell the truth anymore, and I'm determined not to give in again, if he asks. It's ridiculous. I don't know how or when he'll explain to Charles, so if you can, try to avoid the subject until I know he has settled things.'

'Will do!'

Joanne laughed softly. 'Are all your evenings next week booked, by any chance?'

'Will you be mad at me if I say they are? I'll be working late a couple of days so that I can finish at lunchtime on

251

Friday, and I'm meeting him on Monday and Wednesday. He's going to an exhibition at someone else's gallery and asked me to go with him, and he's having an exhibition himself of some lesser-known Victorian portrait painter on Wednesday. I've promised to help serve the drinks.'

'No, of course not, silly. We'll get together soon, I'm sure. Enjoy being with him. I really hope you find that he is your love of a lifetime. I can't think of anyone who better suits you.'

'You're a love. We will get together for a natter on the very first day I have free.'

Joanne hadn't put the phone down a couple of minutes before it buzzed again.

'Hello?'

'Hello, Chéri. Adrienne!'

Joanne would have recognized the husky voice just by the accent. 'Hello, Adrienne.'

'I wanted to tell you, that woman was still there when I arrived, but his parents had left. I think Benedict was pleased to see me.'

'Vanessa? Vanessa was still there?'

'Yes, and she has her eyes on Benedict. A blind woman can see that. She is not clever though, and doesn't know Benedict half as well as she thinks. She didn't even realize that buttering Benedict up has an irritating effect on him. I always found that he'd prefer to know that someone dislikes him, rather than that they pretend and flatter to try to impress him.'

The tone of her voice amused Joanne. She clearly hadn't taken to Vanessa either. Joanne listened with interest to her comments.

'I tried to find out what he thought about you. I mentioned I'd met you and we got on. Either he didn't want to say too much in front of Vanessa, or he is being deliberately obtuse for some other reason. He just made the usual kind of non-committal comment. After a while, he started to get impatient and said he had to do some work. He almost threw us out! Not literally, but he made it clear he'd had enough company for one day, and wanted us out of the way. I tried to persuade him to have dinner with Jacque and me tomorrow, but he used the injuries from the accident to put me off. He invited us around for drinks instead. That's just as good.' There was a short pause. 'On the way out with Vanessa, I dropped a hint that you and Benedict might be getting engaged soon. That upset Vanessa, although she tried not to show it.'

'You did what? Adrienne, you know that isn't true.'

'I know that, and you know that, but I couldn't help myself. She is an annoying woman.'

'I hope that Benedict never gets to hear of it. He'll strangle you!'

'Oh! I have the feeling Vanessa is too much of a coward to ask Benedict if it is true or not. She'll stew in her own juice for a while, and that's not a bad thing. She is one of these arrogant people who have never done a decent day's work in their lives and still expects everyone to adore them.'

Joanne chuckled. 'Perhaps, but that doesn't give you the right to destroy all her dreams. She may end up as Benedict's wife one day, and then you'll find yourself in a real pickle.'

'She's not Benedict's type. She is a woman who has nothing to do with real life. She'd bore Benedict to death in no time at all.'

'Well, I hope that there won't be any repercussions, for your sake. To be honest, I'm hoping that this ridiculous situation will be cleared up soon. I hope that Benedict will tell everyone I've been dispatched to the far corners of his life and his memory for evermore. Then I can get on with my life again, without wondering what can go wrong next. I don't like living a lie.'

Adrienne paused. 'I'm not sure if you are being honest with yourself, Joanne. Do you really want him to forget you? Do you never want to see him again? Think hard about that before you make that

kind of statement. Bye, Chéri! Take care.
I hope we'll meet again sometime.'

'Bye, Adrienne. Thanks for the information.'

There was a click and the connection was broken.

11

The next couple of days were uneventful. Sally returned to work and Joanne was free to concentrate on her office work again. One afternoon, she went round to update Mrs Prothero on how the company stood, and its future prospects. After she'd given her the gist of things, Joanne spent a delightful couple of hours, drinking tea and hearing about her boss's cat.

She looked forward to going to work every day for the first time in months. There were no petty arguments about who was responsible for what, no unfair recriminations about the occasional mistakes that happen in every job now and then. Bill and Sally were good workers and they'd accepted her. She was free to consider ways of improving their system and expanding business. It was wonderful to have the freedom to make decisions, without fighting someone to do so.

Thursday morning, she set out for work as normal, following the usual route. On the way, she always passed a newsagent, and depending on the time, she sometimes stopped to buy something. As she was walking past this morning, she was drawn to the thick, large lettering of the billboard, advertising the headlines of one of the national newspapers. Her stomach lurched as she read the words 'Multi-millionaire Benedict North's love affair'.

For a moment she thought she was going to be sick. She went inside, grabbed a copy and threw some money haphazardly on the counter before retreating fast. The owner looked at her with surprise, because she was a regular who normally exchanged a friendly word. He shrugged; everyone had their bad days.

Joanne walked on for a couple of minutes, the newspaper gripped tightly in her hand. She was almost afraid to stop and read the article. In the end, she halted in a quiet part of the street and opened the paper at the appropriate place. She could soon tell the article was clearly aimed to be sensational rather than informative. She was exceedingly relieved that they didn't mention her name in full, or how she and Benedict had first met. Either they didn't know, or they were planning to deliver more garish details in a follow-up article. There was a photo of Benedict, but not one of her. She was merely referred to as Miss C. The journalist reported that Miss C was currently using all her talents to trap one of the UK's richest and most eligible bachelors into an engagement. It also stated that it was surprising that a man who was such a shark in the business world could be so easily misled by a shapely figure and a pretty face.

She paled and felt a moment of panic. What could she do to contest the article? It made her sound like she was an avaricious harpy with one aim in life — to catch Benedict. They hadn't printed her actual name, but somehow she felt they knew it. The fact that they'd only used an initial in this article meant it would be impossible to start libel charges or refute outright what was written. Benedict could do something though; he was named in full. She was certain he'd put his legal department onto it straight away. Prominent people often faced situations such as this, and she presumed Benedict was no stranger to such occurrences.

She crumpled the paper and walked on. When she arrived, Bill and Sally were surprised by her brief greetings. They had got into the habit of having a quick chat over the first coffee of the day and reviewing what was expected that day. This morning, after a brief greeting, Joanne left them abruptly, telling them she had something important to do, and they were free to sort everything out to best suit themselves. If they'd had the chance to study her face more carefully, they might have noticed the tight lines around her mouth and the worried expression in her eyes.

She knew that Benedict would call,

and she barely had time to hang up her coat before he did. She tried to pull herself together when she noted it was his number on the display.

'Hello, Benedict.'

His voice sounded dangerously calm. 'Have you seen the papers this morning? There's an article about us.'

'Yes. It's offensive, isn't it? I expect you are used to this kind of thing. I'm not. I wondered if I could do anything to stop it, but my name isn't really mentioned, so I have no legal recourse, do I?'

'I've put my people on to it, but I'm just wondering where they got the information in the first place. These kinds of reporters are leeches, and they use anything they think is juicy news to fill their columns. There is nothing particularly damning in what they wrote, but there is one interesting detail — the reference to Miss C. Where did that come from? We haven't been seen out together much publicly, apart from that first evening.' There was a pause. 'They didn't mention where the information came from, but it's clearly inside information. Only the people involved know.'

It took a second for her brain to kick in, and then she said, 'I hope you are not suggesting I had something to do with it? I would hardly portray myself in this light, in the gutter press, to attract you, would I?'

He drawled, 'You'd be surprised by the sort of things that some women do to catch my attention.'

She drew a deep breath and felt her annoyance increasing. She found that her hands were shaking, and at the same time, misery tightened like a steel band around her heart.

She swallowed hard and buried her anger long enough to retort, 'Know something, Benedict? You are the meanest, most deplorable person I've met. The fact that you could believe I had anything to do with that article is enough to make me wild. You can tell the newspaper what you like, but I would be grateful if you could keep my full name out of it, so that I can forget you, and the whole business, and get on with my life. Going to the agency that day was the stupidest thing I've ever done. It's brought me nothing but trouble. Please don't bother me again, for any reason. I've had enough!' She cut the connection and felt the tears finding their path down her cheek.

Her phone rang again and she saw it was his number. Her thoughts about him were too jagged and too painful. She took the receiver off the hook for a while. She tried in vain to carry on with a normal day's work, but found she kept entering things in the wrong places, and making constant typing errors. She wished she could be alone with her thoughts. She could no longer deny that she loved him, but he didn't deserve her love — if he'd ever wanted it, which he didn't.

By the end of the day, she had a headache. She used it as an excuse to leave a little earlier than usual. Bill nodded. He knew that something was wrong — her eyes were puffy and her nose was red — but she didn't go into details about whether she was ill, or if there was some other reason, and Bill was diplomatic enough not to ask too many questions.

She walked home silently, still grappling with the hurt and the inevitability of the situation. The wind was blustery and the sky was a leaden colour. It suited her mood perfectly. Daylight had almost faded by the time she reached her flat and climbed the steps with a heavy heart.

She was glad to be in the comfort of her own surroundings, and after hanging up her coat she knew she wouldn't be able to eat. She couldn't concentrate either and the evening stretched endlessly ahead of her. She needed to think of other things; anything but Benedict North. Joanne's Gran had always said, 'If something's bothering your head, keep your hands busy.' She grabbed the basket of waiting ironing. She thought about her Gran, about her family, about Colleen; she tried making plans for her next holiday — anything to avoid thinking about

Benedict. Now and then, for a second or two, she was almost successful. The familiar movement of the iron did help a little. She had to concentrate on not burning something. She still felt an acute sense of loss, even though he had never been hers to lose. It felt impossible to accept he was now an episode in her past — but that's what she had to achieve.

The doorbell interrupted her thoughts. She was apprehensive but opened it a little and peeped through the gap. It was Benedict. He looked irritated. The wind was blowing his dark hair haywire. The soft material of his coat, swirling around his lean form, was witness to the hostility of the weather. His arm was still in a sling, but Joanne noticed he wasn't using a crutch, so his knee must be a lot better.

She took an automatic step back when she recognised him, but she kept the chain on the door. Her voice was cold and exact.

'What do you want?'

'We need to talk.'

She shook her head. 'What is there to talk about? I'm finished with the whole thing, Benedict. I'm tired of your recriminations, of falling in line with your wishes, and of hearing you tell me I'm the source of your problems.'

He ran his hand down his face, and then, with a stern-faced expression, he said, 'I've never said you were the source of my problems. Look, can I come inside so that we can sort this out?'

'No, you can't. You don't seem to understand that I don't want to see or speak to you again. You can tell the press, your friends and your parents whatever you like. I don't care. Just leave me alone.' She made to close the door in his face. He stepped forward and put his foot in the gap. There was a lump the size of Everest in her throat, but somehow she managed to say, coldly and quietly, 'Take your foot out of the way; otherwise I'll call the police.'

A look of discomfort and then one of withdrawal crossed his face.

'I'll leave, but I want you to know

that I was not accusing you of anything this morning. You jumped to the wrong conclusion straight away. I've tried to phone you several times, but you've blocked my number. That's why I came this evening. I want you to know that I have set the wheels in motion to find out where they got their information from, and I'll do all I can to keep your name out of it. That's if they have any intention of writing some kind of follow-up story.'

She glowered at him. 'A suggestion from me: tell your company lawyers to tell them that we had a passing affair. We know it wasn't even that, but they don't. A newspaper isn't likely to make a fuss about a past relationship, unless both people are social stars, and I'm certainly not one, am I?'

'I want to know where they got their information from in the first place. There's no point in me making a statement when I don't have the details. If I make the wrong kind of denial, they'll fall on me like a ton of bricks. I don't know what they have on us at present. If I say we've had an affair, it infers we've been together a long time, and we haven't. If I deny ever meeting you, they already know that's a lie. If I say we're still getting to know each other properly, it works contrary to our intention of terminating things. To avoid bad publicity for me — and you, if they know your name — I have to find out exactly what they know, and who told them. Then I can react accordingly.'

Just looking at him now made her feel she could die for one of his smiles. She felt ice spreading through her stomach when she began to think that this would probably be the last time she would ever see him in person.

'Then I can only wish you luck, and hope you're satisfied with the findings. I had nothing to do with it. I have never had plans to trap you into anything. I wanted the whole business to stop a long time ago. You were the one who kept finding excuses to keep up the pretence. I wouldn't know how to manipulate you.

I've known from the start that you are someone who can't be manipulated.' His eyes looked empty and the skin tightened over his cheeks as she continued, 'I just want to get on with my life again, as if we'd never met. If I'd found my present job just a couple of weeks earlier, we never would have — and that would have been better for both of us, because we live in two different worlds.'

With a hard edge to his voice, he said, 'You talk as though you hate me.'

'Hate you? No, why should I? I've never hated you — but I don't understand you. You have walls around you five feet thick, and anyone who comes close gets hurt. The only people you seem to care about are your mother, Charles and Vanessa. I don't want to be the target for your gunfire anymore.'

She felt, rather than saw, his shocked expression. Without replying, he turned on his heel and went down the steps. Joanne closed the door and turned to rest her back against it. She slid down its rough surface and landed up sitting on the floor, with her legs stuck out in front of her. She lifted her hands to her face and began to cry. She felt utterly devastated, even though she'd wanted to make a final break, and had managed it. It was one of the moments she was glad she lived alone. There was no one else around to see her misery, or offer pointless consolation.

* * *

Joanne wished she could phone Colleen and pour out her troubles, but last time they'd spoken, Colleen had been bubbling over with happiness because she thought she'd found Mr Right at last. She was in love with Charles, and it sounded like he was with her. Joanne decided this was not the right moment to intrude on the special time they were having together with her gloom and despair. It could wait.

She spent one of the unhappiest nights of her life. She had a feeling of emptiness and desolation. He didn't know what she felt for him, no one did. Added to the wretchedness was the feeling that she hadn't really given him the chance to explain in the way he wanted to last night. Quibbling on the doorstep was no fair solution. Thinking about it now, as she stared above her bed at the darkness of the ceiling, she had to admit that someone like him, in his kind of position, didn't make an apology to anyone very often, and that was what he'd tried to do, clumsy as it was. She'd just chosen to ignore it.

Next morning, she had no energy and felt completely wrung out. She'd only fallen into an exhausted sleep for a few hours before it was time to get up and get ready for work. The bathroom mirror showed her white face and emerging dark rings under her green eyes. Even the green seemed darker and more subdued this morning. She brushed her burnished hair determinedly and focussed her thoughts on getting through the day ahead. Forcing herself to drink something before she left, she pushed aside her untouched bowl of cornflakes and set out for work as usual. The fresh air helped her muddled thoughts a little, and she tried concentrate on other things as she went along. She couldn't afford to think of Benedict in any way, otherwise the tears might start falling again, and it was time for her to pull herself together.

At work, Bill was already helping to unload a delivery with the van's driver. He gave her a passing glance and said good morning. He tilted his head.

'You look bushed this morning. Are you okay?'

Joanne managed a weak smile. 'I do have a bit of a headache, but I'm alright. Is Sally in?' She turned away in the direction of the stairs.

'Yes, she's out back. You don't look okay to me. Hope you haven't caught Sally's bug.'

'I'm fine, Bill. I'll be down for a cup of coffee later on.'

Watching her for a couple of seconds, he scratched the side of his head and then turned back to helping with the delivery.

The morning dragged. She checked the post and made appropriate piles. She was glad to have something sensible to do, even if she had to concentrate hard. She stuck to her routine and even managed to share a coffee with the other two. If she didn't join in as much as usual, the others didn't comment, and she was grateful for that.

Things were up to date, and the afternoon dragged. She started thinking about gathering information and photos to make a new brochure for their customers. Nothing had been done to attract new customers for quite some time, and Joanne planned to make an attractive flier — something to reassure old customers that they were keeping up-to-date, and perhaps encourage new customers to try them out. Looking at the wall clock, she bundled some of the information into a folder and closed the computer down. Downstairs, she stuck her head round Bill's door briefly. He was sitting with his feet up on the desk, reading something.

'Bill, I'm off. I'm taking some work home with me. My headache is getting worse.'

He nodded understandingly. 'Do that. You don't look too good. Perhaps a rest over the weekend will sort you out. You shouldn't bother about taking work home, if you feel bad.'

She smiled. 'It's not that bad. I won't need to have a conscience about leaving a bit earlier if I take something home.'

He laughed gruffly. 'You don't need a bad conscience, you've settled in well and already run this place like clockwork. I'll check everything before I lock up.'

When Joanne got home, she put the kettle on for a cup of tea and spread the information on the desk she'd built in the niche under the stairs. It was compact, but served its purpose well. After eating a bowl of soup, that tasted surprisingly good, she settled down to work. She didn't notice the time pass and when she looked at her watch next, she was surprised to see it was gone six and already dark outside. She thought briefly about going home over the weekend, but it was already too late for that. It wouldn't be worth it.

The doorbell broke the silence and continued to ring at persistent intervals. She gave in, and went to open it. Her heart catapulted upwards as she saw Benedict's familiar features. It wasn't so stormy this evening, but the wind still managed to ruffle his hair.

He held up his free hand. 'Before you slam the door in my face again, give me the chance to tell you what I've found out about that newspaper article. Charles said I shouldn't give up talking to you, and even though I haven't had to do anything like this before, I'm asking you to give me a chance and listen to what I have to say.'

'This has nothing to do with Charles.'

'I told him the truth about us. He was surprised, of course, but more surprised that we can't sort out our differences like intelligent people. He told me he understood why you are angry, but that I should come here again and give it another try.'

She swallowed hard and met his eyes without flinching. Joanne guessed she looked a fright. She hadn't even brushed her hair since she'd arrived home. She ran her fingers through it, then removed the chain on the door and waved him inside. He looked suitably surprised, but didn't need a second bidding. Joanne closed the door behind him, and he stood aside so that she could walk ahead of him into the living room.

He looked around. 'Nice!'

Just seeing him in her flat made her heart skip a beat. It was ridiculous. She lifted her chin. 'Not dockland standard, I'm afraid. Most of what you see here comes from Ikea.'

'Nothing wrong with Ikea. Ingvar Kamprad is a man after my own heart. Do you know what he's worth? And he started out from scratch.'

Joanne didn't want him to stray too

far from the subject at hand.

'I presume you've found out the source of the information for that newspaper article?'

'Yes. Well, actually, our legal department did. I told them to investigate.'

'And?' She crossed her arms across her slight frame and waited.

'They discovered that Vanessa had passed on scraps of information about us to a journalist over a cosy cup of coffee. She didn't take any money for it, so it's clear that she was doing it for a completely different reason.'

Her eyes widened. 'Vanessa? She's one of your oldest friends, isn't she? Why would she do that?'

'I thought she was a friend, but putting two and two together, I think as soon as you came onto the scene, she started to get edgy because she had other plans for me.'

She was too startled not to retort, 'Because she was hoping to end up as more than a friend?'

He didn't look smug or even

surprised; he just shrugged and looked a little sad.

'Presumably. I haven't asked her why she did it, and don't think I'll bother to confront her personally either. I just want her to keep out of my sight. Once she realizes I know she was behind it, she'll bury her head in the sand and hope the bushfire passes over her without too much damage, but I never want to see her again. Charles was shocked enough to say he'll ignore her too. I can't forgive her. A real friend wouldn't have done that. She had no reason to ever believe I thought of her in a romantic way. Apparently, she told the reporter that she'd heard you and I were on the brink of getting engaged, but she'd met you and decided you were a gold-digger, after my money and my social standing. She told him it would make a good article if he wrote something to show me how avaricious you were, before it was too late. Of course, he was glad to have a juicy bit for the social column, especially as in this case, it was free. He knew Vanessa's name, but promised he wouldn't reveal his source. That only worked until our legal department started to put pressure on his editor-in-chief.'

'She must have been at the end of her tether, and desperate to hold on to you,' volunteered Joanne.

'Don't give Vanessa a second thought. Adrienne mentioned to me how she'd met Vanessa and you. I had her and Jacque over for drinks, and she told me how she'd had fun annoying Vanessa with the news I was about to get engaged. That's typical of Adrienne! She always rushes in where angels fear to tread, just for kicks.'

Joanne nodded at Benedict silently. It would seem that, with her fabrication, Adrienne had unwittingly set off the chain of events that had led to all of this. Joanne hadn't liked Vanessa enough to try and let her know the truth — perhaps Vanessa wouldn't have gone to the press if she had.

She said emphatically, 'I like Adrienne.

She's impulsive and unpredictable and full of energy. I don't think she's deliberately unkind.'

'Don't underestimate her. Adrienne can be quite spiteful if she doesn't like someone, so don't ever believe she's a tactful, loving creature. I'm not saying she sets out to be unpleasant — she's just sublimely thoughtless. She's absolutely exhausting too. That was the main reason our relationship didn't last long. We lived in two different worlds. She didn't have much sympathy for the demands of my work, and I never felt really happy in the round of endless parties she needed all the time. Our meetings were few and far between, otherwise it wouldn't have lasted as long as it did.'

One part of Joanne was curious enough to listen to him, and the other part felt jealous when she heard him talk so candidly about his affair with Adrienne. She couldn't help herself, and asked, 'Isn't it strange to see her again, now that she's married and has a little girl with another man? After you'd been so close?'

His mouth twitched with amusement. 'No, not really. I soon realized I wasn't in love with her, and Adrienne didn't grieve when it finished either. She's happy with her present husband; they are similar characters. Jacque is always on the go. He is extremely outgoing. It doesn't bother him that his wife had a past before she met him.'

Meeting his glance she retorted, 'Why should it? From what I hear, your lifestyle has always been quite colourful too. Why should you condemn women when your attitude hasn't been ascetic either?'

His eyes were full of humour. 'Don't believe all the rubbish that is written in the press. True, I haven't lived the life of a monk, but I'm in my mid-thirties, and it would be unusual if I hadn't met some attractive women along the way and enjoyed their company. I have never felt a serious attraction to any woman, up until now — and I never pretended otherwise whenever I spent time with any woman. I didn't realize I was looking for someone until recently. Suddenly, I found out I wanted dependability, honesty, intelligence, and someone who had a hell of a lot of patience with me, and the way I acted. I found out, in the last couple of weeks, that I need . . . you.'

She stopped breathing and the ground under her feet seemed to tilt. She wondered if she'd heard properly. She had a giddy feeling in her stomach. He was saying he liked her.

He continued determinedly, 'And if you didn't already have a boyfriend, I'd fight for you.'

She managed to gather enough sense to utter, 'What boyfriend?'

'The one I met the evening I came to pick you up, when we went down to Charles' for the weekend. The one you telephoned when we were there.'

Puzzlement spread across her features as she tried to recall what he was talking about, then she smiled, as realization dawned. 'Do you mean David?'

A shadow of annoyance crossed his face. 'Yes, that was the name. David.'

'David is my brother!'

'What?' He ripped the word out and stared at her silently for a second. 'Do you mean to say I have been fighting devils and losing sleep, just because I misunderstood? I've wanted to tell you what I felt several times, but I resisted because I remembered how relaxed you seemed with David when I saw you together. I have my principles about trying to pinch someone else's girl-friend. I also loved you enough to want you to be happy, even though it wasn't with me. I didn't imagine for a moment he could be a relative. I should have asked some questions and saved myself the unhappiness, shouldn't I? Please tell me there isn't any other man in your life! Is there?' He reached out, grabbed her hand and pulled her toward him.

She took in every detail of his features. She felt the hardness of his body and his warm breath on her face. He brushed a gentle kiss across her forehead before his mouth covered hers and devoured its softness. His plastered arm was in the way, but she didn't intend to let that bother her. She was almost shocked at her own eager response and she returned his kiss with reckless abandon. All the longing for him bubbled up from within, and she had never felt so happy.

He drew back for a moment and gave a jubilant laugh.

'To think how miserable I've been, imagining that you belonged to someone else. You do like me a little, don't you? Your kiss tells me so, but I've never wanted someone so badly, and I think my judgement is not as rational as it should be.'

'Of course I like you, but I haven't always liked you so much as I do now.' He tilted his head to consider her carefully. 'In fact, I almost disliked you, now and then. You are so bossy, so unsympathetic, so intolerant sometimes.'

His eyes twinkled. 'I know. It's my usual method of keeping myself under control. I thought I didn't stand a chance of winning you over, so I decided the best thing was to push you out of reach by behaving badly. But whenever I did, I couldn't stand the thought of not seeing you again, and I'd start planning how I could. Can you forgive me? Do I have a chance that you do love me a little?'

She nodded and felt the euphoria taking over her whole being.

'I do, and I have done for a while now. I don't know when it happened, or why. I didn't even want it to, it just did.' She hesitated for a moment, then said, 'Benedict, if you are considering me as some kind of fleeting adventure, please stop now. I don't want to be a footnote in your history. With me, it's all or nothing. We don't know if this is a temporary attraction or not, but I'm not intentionally looking for a short-lived escapade.'

He kissed her again. 'I know that. Do you think I want something else?' He shook his head, in answer to his own question. 'This time, it's for keeps.'

From the expression in his eyes and

on his face, to the feelings he generated in her, Joanne savoured every moment. The kiss sent the pit of her stomach into a wild swirl. She couldn't believe what was happening.

He took her hand and pulled her towards the couch. He pulled her onto his lap and slipped his arm around her waist. 'I never thought I would fall in love. Not real love, like I feel for you. I want to spend my life with you, and I want to grow old with you. I've never felt that for any other woman I've met before.'

She considered him carefully. 'Benedict, we don't really know each other, do we? Up until now, we have always been playing a part when we were together. Perhaps we are kidding ourselves about something. Perhaps what we feel at the moment won't last. Love, real love, isn't just pretending or mere physical attraction.'

He viewed her buoyantly. 'I know all that, but I also know that just being with you gives me intense pleasure. More than I've ever known before in my life.

In the last couple of weeks, my concentration on business has been continually disrupted because I kept wondering where you were, what you were doing, and what new excuse I could find to see you again. I felt a special kind of magnetism between us from the very first evening. I loved you even when you disapproved and were telling me off. Especially then. Even if I kept acting like a bear with a sore head, in reality I was thinking what an amazing person you were to be with. You have never been impressed by what I stand for, by my possessions, or the prominent side of my life. I kept thinking, why the hell have I met this woman too late? But I haven't, have I?'

The colour had returned to her cheeks and her eyes sparkled again. 'No, it's not too late, but we have to take things step by step. Your work could come between us. You have responsibilities I know nothing about. I don't know if I could cope with that kind of life.'

'There's only one way to find out! We have to give it a try. If you want to get involved in my work and my public life, okay. If not, it's okay by me too. In fact, I can imagine I'll be content to share a life with you that has nothing to do with my businesses, if that's the way you want it to be. I do know that you are beautiful and you have the gift of making people like you. I can't wait to have you at my side. You will make everything from here on in worthwhile, if you give us the chance.'

'I've never been accused of that particular gift before! Vanessa couldn't stand me, and all through my life there have been people who thought I was employing my looks to get on, instead of my brains.'

Breaking into a broad smile he kissed her again. 'They were jealous! Perhaps I should buy your company, then you'll be safe from any future job loss.'

'Don't you dare! I'm going to make it a going concern, on my own!'

He threw back his head and let out a peal of loud laughter that encouraged her to join in. Then they viewed each other in silent contentment, and both of them wondered what they'd done to end up with such a perfect partner.

He said quietly, 'Many people walk in and out of your life. But only someone you really love leaves a footprint on your heart. You, my love, have left a permanent one on mine!' He threw his free arm round her shoulder and looked around. 'This is the best place I've ever been in, and you are the only woman I'll ever love. My life has meaning, at last, and I hope you feel the same?'

She nodded. 'It seems strange that I agree with everything you say, but I do.'

Joanne leaned into his shoulder and Benedict bent to kiss her.

'Once I get rid of this damned plaster next week, nothing will ever come between us again.'

She grinned. 'I can't wait! But some-how I'm sure we'll manage quite well until then!'